THE TOY H

RYLAN JOHN CAVELL

The Toy Hospital	Rylan John Cavell

Dedicated to all the childhood toys we left behind.

The Toy Hospital   Rylan John Cavell

The Toy Hospital				Rylan John Cavell

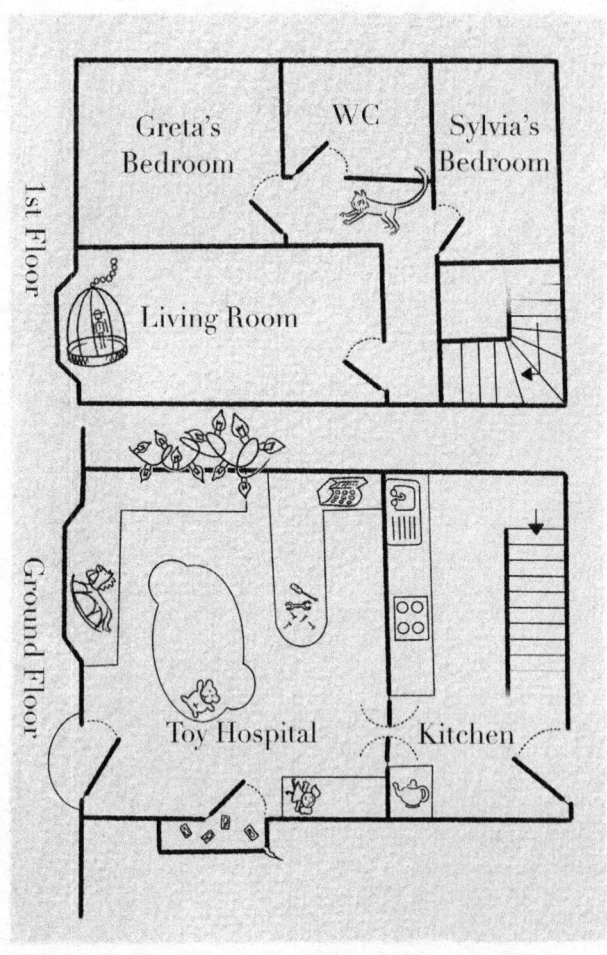

The Toy Hospital					Rylan John Cavell

1 Death By Nursery Rhyme
2 A Gentleman Caller
3 Little Miss Molly Radish
4 Bitter Pudding
5 Break Glass Point
6 The Sorry Tale Of The Tin Soldier And The Troll
7 Fragments
8 The Floral Arrangement
9 Playthings On Parade
10 Just Desserts

The Toy Hospital   Rylan John Cavell

Chapter One
Death By Nursery Rhyme

A pug in a yellow anorak left a fluffy-tummy height trail in the snow as it trotted by its owner's side. At the entrance to a shabby little boutique with a lopsided window the pug cocked its leg.

"Get away with you. I'll have none of that on my doorstep, thank you." Said an ancient woman from the depths of a curly blue-rinsed up-do. She shooed the dog away with the stiff broom with which she was clearing the doorway. Sparkling clouds of frigid snow and ice swirled before her as she set vigorously to her work. The pug was ushered on, to toilette elsewhere.

Pausing briefly, she leaned on the shaft of the broom, and took in the picture-postcard scene. Thomas Street was usually buzzing with early morning coffee drinkers, business people yakking loudly into their newfangled mobile telephones, cyclists jostling for priority with taxis, and occasionally one or two sorry states still making their way home from the night before. Greta

Pudding curiously examined the strange new sound that the snow storm had brought to Manchester; Silence.

From the front of her teetering establishment, she usually felt the world was at her doorstep. She loved the hurly-burly of city life, while maintaining her calm hurricane's eye. That eye was the shop whose doorstep she had paused the sweeping of. And it wasn't any old run-of-the-mill shop. It was a toy shop. But more than that, even. It was a toy hospital. She was very proud of the work she did within the dark and crooked walls of her establishment.

Today, the world at her doorstep was held at arm's reach. It was just a hop further than she could make with her crunchy old knees. Overnight, the streets of Manchester had been taken by surprise by the icy storm. Gritters went out too late, doing only half a job before having to give up and take shelter. Blowing sideways, striking the city at acute angles from the nearby Pennines, the storm had sprung from nowhere, and when it was done, it went back off to nowhere. Roads were smothered. Pavements were coated.

Doorways were inundated. A very odd snow-storm indeed; It had intention, and malice. It clawed at letterboxes, sanded sharp angles to pumice curves, and set with murderous intent at the statues and spires of the city skyline. The rattling of window panes had woken Greta and her business partner Sylvia Garland, who both dwelt above the shop. They had huddled together overnight, basking in the warmth of the electric fire in their pokey living room, where they watched the blizzard attack the street. They heard at least one window break. Thankfully, it wasn't one of their own.

Sylvia felt the cold more acutely, despite being in possession of a sturdily padded frame. Like an old armchair, she was comfy and patterned and welcoming. Greta, on the other hand, was frail and spindly, and shorter by a head than her friend. Her joints protested like an old gate, and she was barbed as the rusted nails that held together her rickety frame.

"A very odd snow-storm indeed." Sylvia had said, as she pulled a blanket around her sturdy shoulders. Hot cocoa had soothed them, eventually, back to the land of nod.

From the doorstep, broom in hand, Greta examined the glistening white icing with a squint of her spectacled eyes. She was suspicious of it. The sweet confection of the day hid the grime, and the grey, and the red-brick dust belly of the beast. The sky was a pale blue dome, and entirely absent of clouds.

"A very odd snow-storm. Indeed." Intoned Greta, soaking up the silence.

Greta had not had an easy life. Troublesome people seemed drawn to her, and over the years she had grown a hard shell, like a wrinkled walnut, to keep herself safe. She had become known by some as a curmudgeon. By others a survivor. By some, in somewhat more unsavoury terms. But whatever they called her, it bothered her not one jot. She knew herself very well, and would not permit the opinion of others to dent her worth.

She made her way through the shop front of her toy hospital, admiring her handiwork. Rescued rocking horses galloped in still-life upon their curved rockers. Recombobulated puppets hung from waxed strings, not a tangle in sight, and merry with rosy painted cheeks. Teddies with paisley neckerchiefs, dollies that blinked when you laid them down, wind-up waddling ducks, and perfectly fitting nesting dolls. All of these and more adorned the rippling shelves fixed to the walls, and the atolls that sprung up here and there from the worn sea-blue carpet.

The only person in all her life who could see beyond that uncrackable exterior, and into the soft, squashy Victoria sponge that was truly Greta Pudding, was her life-long friend and business partner. Sylvia emerged from the little back room with a fresh pot of tea, and the pockets of her tabard stuffed with tiny tools. She jingled as she walked. Sylvia was the nurse to Greta's doctor. But today there was no surgery planned. Still, Sylvia was prepared for an emergency. Eyes and noses and buttons could come away from old and much-loved cuddly toys at any moment! The toy hospital would always be ready.

"It's the first of December." Sylvia said. She attempted to sound casual. It was a significant date in both their lives, and never passed without incident.

"I'm aware," Greta clattered their chipped and familiar mugs from beside the mechanical cash register, and presented them, "and I'm gasping."

The tea was served with lemon and honey, and the two of them sipped in companionable silence.

"What'll it be this year?" Sylvia asked eventually.

Greta finished her tea and placed the mug down firmly as answer. They both knew what would happen that evening. Well, they had an inkling.

"Come along, Greta." Sylvia cooed, "We know what he's up to, after a fashion. If we put our heads together we can put a stop to it. Maybe not for good, but for today at least." Sylvia had always been the optimist of the two.

"Cats." Greta spat. "This year it'll be cats."

"So what do we do?"

"We do nothing." Greta scowled behind her oversized horn-rimmed glasses, "He's my itch to scratch. You just keep yourself cosy in your bed tonight. I'll deal with him."

Sylvia mushed her lips together in consternation. Her friend had always been one to play the martyr, always taking burden best shared, solely onto her own thin shoulders. Every year, despite Sylvia's pleas otherwise, Greta's walnut carapace would harden as the dread date edged closer. The first of December this year marked the fourth anniversary of the demise of Pevril Pudding; Greta's husband.

Sylvia thought back to those early months of Greta's widowdom. What should have been a breath of fresh air and a clean start for her best friend was anything but. Did that brute slip quietly into the night? No. No, he did not. Pevril Pudding had been a rough and hot-tempered sort in life, and it seemed that he kept his ill temper into the grave, and out again.

Sylvia had moved in a few months after his passing, taking up the box bedroom above the toy hospital, at the back, overlooking the yard and the alley that hid there. But even in death that oafish man liked to throw his weight around, though of course in his new situation, he was much less able to leave bruises as evidence.

As the first anniversary of his death had approached, bumps in the night grew bumpier, the things in the corner of their eyes became thingier, and the spooky shadows at their backs ever spookier! They could tell something was happening, they knew in their bones that something was coming.

That first year it was flies. Somehow a swarm of flies was conjured into Greta's bedroom, where they buzzed, thick as molasses around her head, trying to force their way into her nose and mouth. Shrieking and spitting, Greta had hid under her duvet, flailing and squirming, trying to seal herself up tight in the covers. She hid there wailing until the buzzing had ceased. Sylvia had come to the rescue armed with the bug zapper from the kitchen. As Greta's hair-netted head appeared cautiously from the safety of the covers, Sylvia switched off the glowing trap and sniffed, saying "I'll get a dustpan and brush."

The swarm was swept up and disposed of. Sylvia thought abstractly how the tiny dead bodies looked like raisins, until one of the little beasts twitched its wings, and she slammed the lid of the bin shut tight.

The next year was spiders. On the night of the first of December they wove a cocoon around poor Greta's bed while she slept; a million spindly, hairy legs silently tip tapped across the cotton sheets, weaving their own thick, sticky, smothering shroud. Sylvia had made sure to stay up late, in case of just such an eventuality. But she hadn't counted on spiders. Those wriggly, jiggly, creeping little creatures sent a shiver up her spine.

"Too many knees." She often said of spiders, "They move all wrong. Can't abide 'em."

But she had gulped down her fears, rushing to the aid of her best friend in all the world. A bread knife from the kitchen made short work of the smothering weave, from which Greta erupted like a fountain, gasping and spluttering, sweaty and with a harpy screech. The octopedal assailants scuttled away, vanishing between floorboards, under the skirting board, and away into shadows. That night, even a mug of hot cocoa hadn't soothed Greta's nerves enough to return to sleep.

A week and a half she had slept on the settee in the living room. It hadn't done her back, or her temper, any favours.

"But how do you know it's Pevril's ghost?" Sylvia had asked a very peevish Greta the following year.

"I just do!" Her friend said, grinding her teeth, hunched, and with folded arms, sitting behind the toy hospital counter. They were surrounded by the gaiety of their tinselled Christmas decorations, but feeling none of the cheer, "It's the stupid nursery rhyme he liked to sing at me."

"A nursery rhyme?" Sylvia was mystified. Though she had known a little of Pevril's cruelty, Greta never opened up a great deal, and this was new information, "He sang a nursery rhyme?"

"At me. If ever he found a dead fly, or a spider, or some such thing, wherever he was in the shop, he would creep up on me, singing that damnable ditty, and try to…" She paused, her teeth grinding like mill stones, "He'd try and feed it to me." That's how Greta broke yet another set of dentures.

Sylvia wondered what the song could have been that caused so much torment, and persuaded her dear friend that these odd yearly occurrences were the result of a hateful husbandly haunting.

"There was an old lady who swallowed a fly..." Greta said quietly, "I shan't say the rest out loud. I don't want to encourage the old blaggard."

Sylvia nodded, "It follows." She agreed, "Flies, spiders... then birds?"

Greta folded her arms, "Birds. Tonight I shall be Tippi Hedren."

"I was never fond of that film."

"I'm none too thrilled about reenacting it!"

And indeed she was not, when in the dead of night her bedroom window was flung open, and all manner of malformed and dirty pigeons beat their way inside. Greta found herself cut by claws, and the cold night air. She became entangled in crooked and twitching wings. In this grey storm of feathers and beady orange eyes she spun and wheeled, trying to find the door. They were in her hair, one got up her nightgown, and they obscured her vision. Unable to see which way was which, she stumbled toward the open window, and tripped on a bird flailing on the floor. A barren flower box saved her. Her hands landed upon it, and it fell in her place. It broke apart on the pavement below, scattering a Rorschach blot of dark soil into the road. The birds fluttered over her head, pelting at one another and at her back with their moth-eaten wings to escape. They billowed as a cloud into the night sky, leaving Greta panting against the sill, dishevelled and cursing Hitchcock.

"How absurd, to swallow a bird..." Sang a horribly familiar voice at her back. Instinct took over and she spun around, raising her hands defensively. Pevril was not there... yet he was. A tarnished tin soldier, no bigger than a jar of jam, ran stiffly from the room, singing over its shoulder, "She swallowed the bird to catch the spider that wriggled and jiggled and tickled inside 'er!"

Fear, struck by Greta's iron hammer of will, became rigid fury. She pelted after the toy as fast as her protesting hips and knees allowed. His rattling joints gave him away, as he shuffled awkwardly beneath the arm chair in the living room. She creaked just as loudly as she lowered herself to floor level, and peered under. Rattle rattle rattle! He was off and running again!

"She swallowed the spider to catch the fly!" He sang as he vanished through the living room door, "I don't know why she swallowed the fly..." and thud thud thud, down the stairs, "Perhaps she'll die!"

"Oh no you don't!" Sylvia said, out of sight. She had lain in wait for the night's shenanigans. There followed some banging and thrashing. Then, as Greta finally managed to lift herself upright again, the sturdy shape of Sylvia appeared at the door, wearing oven gloves, clutching a fishing net, and with a souvenir hat from Australia on her head, corks swinging madly on their strings.

"I missed." She said, "And he's vanished off into the hospital somewhere. We'll never find him now."

Greta had forgone the cocoa that night and reached straight for the sherry. She stewed silently, grinding her false teeth, until fatigue overcame her and she began to snore. Sylvia tucked a thick blanket around her, and made sure there was a pot of tea ready the next morning.

"So..." Sylvia mulled over the jellicle connotations, "Tonight it's to be a plague of cats, is it?"

Greta stared across the crowded shop front, through the wonky window and to the brilliant gleaming snow outside. This year felt different. The snow storm and her murderous ex-husband were somehow in cahoots. She knew it.

Pouring herself a second mug of tea, she sighed, "I've work to do, Sylv. All this hocum is nothing but a bother. This rocking horse won't mend its own leg, will it!"

"It's a little more than a bother, Greta! You've a ghost trying to finish you off with a nursery rhyme!"

Greta shooed her friend away, "Leave me be, you old fusspot."

Sylvia knew that when a conversation was ended by Greta Pudding, there was no resuscitating it. She left a handful of the tools from her jangling tabard pocket on the counter top, and shuffled away into the back room, where their kitchen was huddled in one dim corner. It was while she stood there, dunking a ginger-nut biscuit into her brew that an idea came to her. She smiled, and chortled a little, which gained her a very suspicious glare from Greta.

A few minutes later, biscuit and brew forgotten, Sylvia was off wading through the snow up Thomas Street on a mission. Greta watched her go, and shook her head. Her friend was prone to flights of fancy and whimsy. No doubt she would be regaled with a tall tale of city-centre adventure upon her return.

As her gaze lingered on the bright square of the front window, the pug and its owner made their way back the way they had come. Once more the little dog paused and cocked its leg.

Greta rushed forward, "None of that on my step, if you please!" She shouted through the glass of the door, startling the dog's owner.

Greta stewed behind the toy hospital counter, and found herself unable to focus on the lame rocking horse. The rickety thoroughbred was not due for collection until the following week, so she had time. It was simply something to do to occupy her mind. Yet it failed. Each time she picked up a tool, it wasn't the right one, or she couldn't quite get a good angle on the leg, or her back ached a little too much, or her knees demanded a rest. Furious, she threw down the tools.

"This just won't do at all!" She fumed to herself. Each year she became a hysterical mess, when beset by nursery rhyme beasts. Never before in her life had she ever screamed, or wailed, or even whimpered. Not even when Pevril was at his most vindictive and brutal. She was sensible, rational, dogmatic, pragmatic, and lots of other things folk said in hushed tones which she suspected weren't at all polite. Yet for the last three years, each December the first night, she had been reduced to a snivelling, skriking, shrieking shambles, "Not this year." She told herself resolutely, "And never again."

She did have two things to thank him for, that hateful dead husband of hers; the walnut shell inside which she dwelt, and the toy hospital itself. She closed her eyes, and forced her memories back, back, a long way back, to happier times. She did this whenever the weight of her wounds threatened to bury her, and smother her in melancholy.

As a marriage should start, theirs did; with love. Romance, and his strong arms both swept her off her kitten-heeled feet. She was quite the snappy dresser in her younger days. Pevril had been sent home from the early days of the War, lame. The shy infatuation of their teenage years blossomed into lust and passion, and they were married on the seventh of September, 1940.

As they exploded together between the sheets, hot in each other's tight embrace on their wedding night, the Luftwaffe drummed a distant accompaniment across the south of the country. The beginning of the Blitz couldn't damage their passion, not even when it arrived on their doorstep and ruined Christmas that same year.

From Pevril's home in Oldham they could see the fires and smoke pouring from the city, a glittering spectacle, hellish and red, dramatic and terrible, glinting and shining like a dreadful festive bauble. Fires burned across Manchester, melting and gurgling, spitting and pluming; a volcano, an open wound, leading straight to Hell. Or so it seemed. But Greta was safe with Pevril. They danced around the living room every evening to their favourite records, safe and warm and occasionally well fed.

But the War following Pevril home had done something to him. Greta didn't see the sadness in his eyes, she ignored the trembling of his hands, finding comfort in his strong arms, as with her head pressed to his chest, they swayed and spun gently about the living room, night after night.

The bombs of her memory sounded suddenly loud and close, and she was snapped from her reverie by Sylvia's bustling return and the slam of the toy hospital door.

"It's quiet as the grave out there." She said, nodding over her shoulder, "Only a few places open. Looks like the snow has blocked all the roads and suchlike. No busses or trams or anything!" She hurried through the shop, leaving a trail of white footprints in her wake, at which Greta scowled.

"What have you got there?" Greta pointed a suspicious finger at the carrier bags slung over Sylvia's arm.

"None of your beeswax." Sylvia grinned, wagging a finger of her own, then vanished into the back room. Greta watched her go, and her gaze followed the sound of Sylvia making her way up the stairs to the first floor, and the click of her bedroom door closing.

"What's that daft mare up to?" Greta mumbled, before turning her attention to the rocking horse once more.

The hours trickled on, and by setting her mind to fixing the toys in her hospital, she quite forgot about the impending attempt on her life. Until, that is, the little clock on the wall cuckooed seven in the evening. So absorbed in the planing of a new rocker for the rocking horse had she been, that the day had quite passed her by. She nodded approvingly at her day's work, and allowed herself a rare smile. It was a pleasant and warm smile, as bright and lovely as her usual expression was frosty and pinched.

Standing up, she uncurled her spine, and groaned as it clunked in several places. She was prone to seizing up. Using her walking stick - which she hated - she made her creaking way to the front of the shop, flipped over the open sign to closed, and locked the door. As she made her way into the back room, she noted how bare and empty their little kitchen was. Sylvia would usually have it filled with dirty pans and the smells of some ungodly stew by now. But the oven was cold, and the pans sat clean in their cupboard. Across the very back wall, arching over the rear door and the kitchen cupboards were the open-sided stairs. Up this mountain trail she hiked, using the wobbly handrail and her stick for support, though she truly didn't ever feel much supported by either.

"I'll go rump over rumple down this staircase one day." She muttered to herself, looking back briefly to base camp.

"What did you say?" Sylvia's head appeared at the top of the stairs. Her cheeks were suspiciously rosy.

"Never mind that, what are you up to? You've no right looking so flushed, hiding away up here doing nothing."

"Ah but I haven't been doing nothing!" Sylvia helped to heave her friend up the last step, and into the narrow landing. There was a bit of business with elbows and bosoms, as Greta attempted to shuffle past.

"Mind where you're..."

"Oh sorry, here..."

"By heck!"

"Beg your pardon!"

"Do you want to know what I've been up to, up here 'doing nothing'?" Sylvia said eagerly.

Eventually Greta navigated around her friend, and through her own bedroom door. She didn't want to linger, she didn't want to sit and chat in the living room as they usually did. She wasn't in the mood.

"Likely best I don't know." Greta said, but had some suspicions. She'd heard about ladies in their time of life suddenly finding new and strange hobbies. Exercise was one she found particularly troubling. All that jiggling about couldn't be good for you, she was sure of it.

"You want me to bring you a mug of cocoa, love?" Sylvia cooed.

"No. Thank you." Greta said as she disappeared from sight behind her bedroom door.

Sylvia sucked her cheek, concern written in bold print across her face. Read all about it, read all about it! She couldn't ever hide her emotions, or her thoughts.

She lingered there a moment, staring at the dark door, before returning to her secretive work. Presently, a loud scraping sound began to emanate from Greta's bedroom.

"Greta?" Sylvia tapped on the door, "Everything hunky dory?"

"As much as you'd expect, given the circumstances." Came the muffled reply.

"What're you up to?"

"Just shifting my furniture about. Having a little rearrangement."

"Feng shui?"

"...What did you call me?"

"No it's…" Sylvia gave up with the muffled conversation, "Never mind."

Greta was not indulging in a spot of evening Feng shui. No. Greta Pudding was building a barricade. In fact, she was building two. One across the door, and another across the window.

"See if you can get your mangy moggies in here now, you horrid little prick." She muttered as she strained, gritting her false teeth. The vanity went in front of the door, and the wardrobe in front of the window. The bed, with its solid metal frame and jangling springs was too much. She puffed and panted, sitting down heavily on her lumpy mattress. She wiped her brow with a handkerchief, and glared about her fortress.

"It'll have to do." She said.

That night she didn't sleep. She pulled up her duvet to make a warm tent for herself as she sat on the edge of the bed and waited. Her dry old muscles were taut like violin strings, and at any provocation she would emit a high C. The flutter of a pigeon alighting briefly on the window ledge startled her half to death. The creak of Sylvia's bed down the hall alarmed her again and again. Greta's ears strained for all sound, any sound, for a warning of what might be coming.

"I hate cats." Greta said to herself, "Pompous, entitled little beggars."

She wanted midnight to come, and for the terror to arrive and be done with. And midnight did come, eventually. She heard the clock downstairs cuckoo the hour. And nothing happened.

Greta realised she'd been holding her breath, and let out a long slow wheeze of relief. Had Pevril finally given up?

Crash! Bang! Wallop! Meow!

The silence was smashed to pieces by the crashing of furniture, doors being slung roughly open, and a million hissing, mewing little voices. Greta let out an involuntary shrill squeak, and pulled her duvet tight about her. She expected her bedroom door to fly open, and the vanity to disintegrate under a thousand razor claws, and be caught in the headlamp glare of a billion yellow eyes! But the sounds that came crashing and bashing and smashing through the toy hospital slowed, faltered, and altered as they reached the landing, and her bedroom door. The hissing subsided. The vicious mewing became purring.

The chill of the night began to vibrate to the thrumm of a un unknowable number of purring cats.

Slowly, Greta relaxed her white knuckles, letting the duvet slip away. What was happening out on the landing? She rose from the bed, inching her way to the barricaded door.

"What have you done!"

Greta stepped back from the door as Pevril's voice broke through the white noise of happy cats.

In response to him, Greta heard Sylvia laughing, and then a series of clattering thuds, followed by a triumphant 'ah-ha'!

"Sylv?" Greta called through the door, "Sylvia?"

Through the sound of contented kitties, she could hear metallic clinking and rattling.

"You can come out now, Greta. I've got him."

As a pale winter dawn rose over Manchester, Greta and Sylvia were sitting in their small living room, staring at a tin soldier in a bird cage.

"So…" Greta began. It had taken her a lot longer to remove the barricade than it had to put it in place, and she was very tired, "How did you…?"

Around them the carpet could not be seen, for the rolling, stretching, squirming bodies of cats. Black cats, tabby Toms, tortoise-shell moggies, mangy old creatures, spry little kittens. More even than T. S. Elliott could have dreamed up.

"Catnip." Sylvia said proudly, "I laced the stairs and landing with it."

That's the mission that had taken her into town earlier that day. A search for catnip. She had trudged through the snow, waist-high in some places, to every shop she could find that sold cat toys, food, and accessories. Everything with catnip in, she bought. She purchased Manchester's entire supply that day.

Back at the toy hospital, while Greta was downstairs grinding her teeth, Sylvia had set to work. She snipped open all the toys and trinkets, ripped open the bags, and ran seams of the stuff through the landing carpet, and around their bedroom door frames.

"I'm surprised you didn't notice the smell yourself, as you went up to bed." Sylvia chuckled.

"I did, in fact, notice it." Greta lied, "But I thought you'd been doing exercise or some similar unhealthy carry-on and that the aroma was you."

Greta was being very snippy. Probably from lack of sleep, Sylvia thought.

"Well once that was done, and you were to bed, all I had do was wait."

And Sylvia had waited very impatiently. She sat on her uncomfortable bed and fidgeted, with oven gloves on, her Australian souvenir hat jammed over her hair, and armed with a fishing net.

Midnight came, Sylvia's eyes had fallen closed with boredom, and she had begun to sleep. She woke abruptly to the crashing and bashing sounds of a tidal wave of cats rolling through the shop downstairs. The wave broke on the stairs, spraying raging balls of feline ferocity into the air. The landing was inundated in moments, and Sylvia gulped hard, clutching the net, as the maleficent moggies began to eye her up, stretching and extending their needle claws. But she needn't have fretted. It took them a few moments to notice the dreamy fragrance, and a few moments more to succumb to its heady powers.

Riding on the back of one of the larger Toms, Pevril kicked and punched at the tamed cats. Then, spotting Sylvia's red, laughing face he knew he was beaten.

"What have you done!" He cried at her, raising his stiff tin arms in the air in a rage.

The net came down on him swift as Sylvia could manage, and she bundled him up into a bag, which was then shoved into an old bird cage.

And that's where Pevril remained, as Sylvia recounted her tale. All the while, Greta stared daggers at the tin soldier, whose emotionless metal face glared back, somehow mocking her.

"What have you got to say for yourself?" Greta asked, keeping as level a voice as she could manage through gritted dentures.

Pevril said nothing.

Chapter Two
A Gentleman Caller

After several hours, the ladies of the Toy Hospital gave up all their attempts at making Pevril answer their questions.

"I don't like the way he just stares at us." Sylvia said, "It's like he's scheming."

Greta agreed, and so they took down the macrame hanger and the cascading Spider plant it cradled from it's hook in the ceiling of their living room, and hung Pevril in its place. The birdcage was only a thin wire thing, but with him locked away, suspended, and then covered with an old table cloth, they felt much better about having him a permanent resident in their home. Knowing that her devilish tormentor was now secure under lock and key, Greta felt a thrill of victory, and she whacked the cage with her walking stick.

"Don't antagonise him!" Said Sylvia, reproachfully.

"Why not?" Greta snapped back, "What's he going to do, trapped in there like a stuffed budgie?"

The oddly mute tin soldier gave Sylvia the willies. If he could seemingly conjure or control flies, spiders, pigeons, and cats... well, what else could he be capable of? And why now remain so silent? What was he up to? He was surely scheming.

The ladies retreated to their rooms as the dawn of the 2nd day of December yawned wide over the city's tower blocks, though neither got much in the way of sleep. Restless, Greta took herself downstairs to the Hospital, flipped the sign and unlocked the door. It wouldn't do, being closed at the start of December. It was their busiest season, after all!

The snow had lingered, but the cats had melted away. One by one the feline intruders had slunk, slithered, and glided away, until only one mangy old tom cat remained. Greta had been thoroughly unable to shoo him away, and so he lounged on the belly of a fat teddy, and watched her with his one good eye.

The smothering white snow seemed almost to have grown overnight, despite the night bringing no further flurries. It was almost knee deep. Usually the start of December was when they did a roaring trade. Christmas presents of restored toys, the fixing of last year's favoured gifts, and browsers usually inundated them and kept them on their toes. But this year the snow kept everyone, bar the most intrepid shoppers, away.

From the depths of a dusty and over-stuffed cupboard, Greta heaved a box that jingled.

"A little festive cheer should lighten the mood." She said to the cat, who flicked his tail and slowly winked. She shook her head, and then her finger, in the cat's direction, "And don't you get any funny ideas about my decorations being toys or scratching posts!"

*

"Careful, now. Don't slip and break another hip!" Sylvia said, finally joining Greta in the Hospital.

The frail, blue-rinsed woman was teetering on the top rung of a thin wooden ladder, stringing tinsel and metallic streamers in zig-zag formations across the ceiling. Sylvia held out a hand, and Greta clasped it as she dismounted.

"Done!" Greta said, pushing her glasses back up her nose.

"You've been busy!" Sylvia grinned, taking in the glitteringly festooned and bedecked Toy Hospital. Greta's blue rinse bobbed as she nodded her satisfaction. It had been a faff, doing it all on her own, but Sylvia had spent the morning in a deep sleep. She seemed very well rested; rosy and plump. Greta glowered under her friend's sunny wakefulness.

"Flick the switch, then. Go on." Sylvia said.

Amongst the tinsel, around the window, and tangled around the plastic tree by the counter, were a galaxy of fairy lights, waiting for the spark of life. Greta reached to the dangerously over-stuffed multi-socket by the cash register and, with a flourish, flicked the switch. Pop. All the lights flashed briefly before going out. Something sizzled as the power died and the two women shrieked in surprise. The tomcat lifted its head to see what the fuss was about.

"Looks to me, you could do with an electrician?" Said a smooth, dark voice from the direction of the door.

"Someone's a smart-alec." Greta tutted, turning and squinting toward the front of the Hospital, "Are you an electrician?" She couldn't make out the features of the man, framed as he was by the bright white of the outside world. He was a silhouette, until he took two slow and carefully placed strides forward.

"Furious Crumpet." He said, as he bowed low.

"I beg your pardon!" Greta spat.

"It's my name." The man rose from his bow.

"Furious?" Greta raised an eyebrow, "What kind of a name is that, when it's at home?"

"It's Italian." The man said, a little too quickly for her liking.

Greta folded her arms, thoroughly unconvinced.

He was tall and handsome, with a square jaw and a light peppering of fashionable stubble. Greta thought his suit looked cheap, but his shoes did not. He had a thick head of black hair, slicked back over his skull, and dark eyes that twinkled like distant lights on the sea, and that hinted at the heat of the Mediterranean summer; Olives and tapas, red wine drunk on hillside terraces, long nights, lazy days and passionate embraces. There was a touch of a young Cesar Romero about him, Greta observed, then shook herself. He had a very powerful effect, and she didn't like that one bit. His dark eyes flicked between the two elderly women.

"I'm looking for..." From under his arm he unfolded a newspaper, flipped to a page near the back and read, "Geriatric Giddy-Up?"

His spell was utterly broken. Before Greta could bark out the string of abrupt syllables she had lined up for this impertinent stranger, Sylvia garbled a series of her own. They were a loud and flustered collection of sounds, none of which made up entire words. Sylvia had gone magenta about the cheeks, and she grabbed at the man's arm and bustled him out onto the street.

Watching them from the rear of the shop, there appeared to be a bit of argy-bargy, Sylvia giving him a mouthful, and him bowing again, then sauntering off. Sylvia held her hand to her forehead, watching him go, then hurried back into the Hospital. She trotted to Greta's side, where she stood silently for a moment, before turning and making herself busy in their little kitchen.

"I'll pop the kettle on." She said.

"You'll be lucky." Greta tutted, eyeing the defunct multi-socket.

"Right." Sylvia banged down the kettle, "No sodding electrickery."

"You want to tell me what all that was about?" Greta said.

"Not particularly."

"I see." Greta adjusted her bust with her folded arms.

"Let's drop it."

"Geriatric Giddy-Up?"

"Greta, no. I said let's drop it." Sylvia wouldn't look at her friend.

"Sylv!"

Sighing heavily, Sylvia turned to face Greta's owl-like gaze. Her usually buoyant form seemed taught, strained, "I'm quite embarrassed." She said, playing with her fingernails.

"We've no secrets, you and I." Greta reached out and took one of Sylvia's hands in both of her own, "Come on. Tell me. Can't promise I won't laugh at you, mind, if you're being a dafty."

Sylvia took a long time to reply, and when she did, Greta's mouth fell open, "You took out a what?" Greta spat, shocked.

"I took out a lonely hearts advert!" Sylvia repeated, pulling her hand back, "Don't look so shocked. I have needs and wants, like any woman."

Greta spluttered, unsure of how to take this information, "And... he... he came here in response to your... advertisement?"

"The way you say it, makes it sound mucky." Sylvia turned away, pulling tea bags from a cupboard, dropping them into the tea pot, and fetching the sugar bowl.

"Isn't it?" Greta still couldn't line up her thoughts, "Advertising for men to call around and see to your 'wants and needs'?"

"It's not like that!" Sylvia went to pour the kettle into the pot, then slammed it down again, "Oh bloody hell."

Greta chuckled, "Well, well, well, Sylvia Garland. You do surprise me. I'll take a look at the fuse box. You calm yourself down before you have some form of fatal palpitation." She wanted to get to the bottom of this, but flustering her friend wouldn't make the truth forthcoming. So, she would let her regain her composure, and probe again later. Which she did.

*

"You likened yourself to a broken rocking horse?" Greta found great amusement in teasing her friend, "Geriatric giddy-up! Indeed!"

Some minor tinkering had restored power to the Hospital, and around them the fairy lights blinked merrily as they poured a pot of tea.

"It didn't sound so silly when I wrote it." Sylvia bemoaned her lack of literary finesse, "but you're only allowed so many words. I had to edit quite a bit out. Suppose it took away much of the context."

"I suppose it did." Greta grinned, and chortled, "But why did you include our address?"

"I didn't."

"So how did whatshisface, Frantic Toast?"

"Furious Crumpet." Sylvia sighed, almost dreamily.

"Yes, him. How did your lothario know to find you here?"

"Search me."

"That's what he was here for, no doubt."

"Eh?"

Greta never enjoyed dishing her friend a home truth or two. The poor love was like a balloon. Easily deflated if you went in too sharply, "A devilishly handsome young man like that? Could have his pick of the girls. Why you?"

"Why not me?"

Greta slurped her tea, "Oh he's nothing but a gold digger! He's here to poke about, case the joint, steal from a naive old biddy and vanish into the night, clicking his heels together like a merry jackalope."

"You don't know that!"

"I know enough. That man means you no good. He gave me a right peculiar feeling. You were correct to put him out. Good riddance, I say."

Sylvia looked away bashfully.

"That is what happened, Sylv? When you and he had words out on the street?"

"After a fashion."

Greta folded her arms and scowled. Sylvia couldn't last long under the pressure of that particular gaze of hers.

"Fine!" she said loudly, "I told him we could go out for dinner tomorrow night."

Greta didn't approve, and made it plain. Phrases such as 'daft old cow', 'silly mare', and other farm animal equivalences were fired at Sylvia. Greta was perhaps more forthright than she would usually have been, lack of sleep having robbed her of patience and tact.

Sylvia became obstinate, and deaf to her friend's protestations out of spite, rather than natural stubbornness, "I don't care what you say,, Greta Pudding! I've not been on a date since nineteen eighty five, and I'm lonely!"

Greta rolled her eyes, which enraged Sylvia further.

"How are you lonely, you've me for company?" Greta said.

"It's not the same, is it?" Sylvia pursed her lips, suddenly realising where the conversation was heading.

"I'm your best friend, Sylvia. What more do you need than me and the Hospital?"

Sylvia shook her head, "Not all men are bad news." Her voice was quiet.

Greta narrowed her eyes, "I never said that."

"But that's what you think. You're a pessimist, when it comes to the opposite sex. I'm an optimist. It's as simple as that."

"You would be too, if you'd lived my life."

"Greta, I don't want to fight." Sylvia said.

"Bit late for that." Greta turned away, and began to heavy-handedly rearrange her tools.

They sulked the remainder of the day away, surrounded by the cheery mess of their Christmas decorations. At some point, the old cat yowled at an old cupboard door, clawing at the carpet in front of it.

"I hate cats." Greta said as she ushered the old tom away from the cupboard door, "Peculiar animals."

3rd of December.

The next morning Sylvia awoke to find the air thick with smoke. Bounding out of bed, she raced downstairs in her nightie and curlers.

"Fire!" she bellowed, "The kitchen's on fire."

From the tangy cloud came a wafted tea towel, "Oh hush your noise and crack the back door open." Said Greta, "It's just a bit of eggy bread gone awry."

With the rear door open, the smoke soon cleared, and Greta's attempt at breakfast found to be the cause.

"But you never cook!" Sylvia said, aghast.

Greta prodded the charred slice into the bin, and shrugged, "Thought I'd make up for being a mard by doing us a spot of brekkie."

Sylvia touched her friend affectionately on the shoulder, "I appreciate the gesture, Greta, but we both know you and cookery don't get on. Let me." And they dined on a mountain of eggy bread, and drank sweet tea, the argument of the previous day forgiven.

Greta had decided that she wouldn't let something as inconsequential as a man get between her and her best friend.

"Men come and go. Women are forever." She often said, when full of sherry. What she meant by that was known only to Greta Pudding.

Inevitably, the subject of Sylvia's impending date reared its head, "I've said my piece on the matter," Greta said to Sylvia as she spritzed a little perfume around the hospital to banish the lingering smell of smoke, "and that's that. I'll not stand in your way. But I'll be here for you when he needs a good arse-kicking. And he will!"

"I thought you'd said your piece?"

Greta opened her mouth to answer back, thought better of it, and mimed zipping her lips shut.

Sylvia hugged Greta, "I know you're only looking out for me. I'm a big girl. I can look after myself."

Greta knew the first two statements to be true, but wasn't so sure about the third.

*

Greta flipped the sign from open to closed, and muttered irritably at the day's lack of customers. She locked the door and made her way back to the counter, where the horse and its new rocker were finally united. The glue was drying, and the nails needed painting over. She was very happy with her work.

Bustling through from the back room, Sylvia did a flustered twirl, "How about this?" It was her third outfit change in half an hour.

Greta pushed her glasses up her narrow nose and scrutinised her friend's outfit. She could have said a lot of things, but she had chosen to be kind and allow Sylvia to do what Sylvia wanted to do, "That's much better." She said, nodding.

"Oh good." Sylvia grinned, her face cracking as the caked makeup creased around her eyes and mouth. She had settled on a black skirt, frilly ivory blouse, and sequinned black cardigan. Her hair was done up in sweeping waves, and she had been very liberal with her Estee Lauder 'Beautiful'.

"You look a treat." Greta said, and meant it. She was much more used to her friend wearing old, itchy skirts, and thick woollen jumpers. She hadn't seen her dolled up in a great many years.

"When was the last time either of us got done up all fancy, eh?" Sylvia asked, "I feel like a teenager again. My heart's all a-flutter!"

Greta shrugged, "I can't recall." She said, truthfully.

"Was it a wedding... or a funeral? One of those foreign cousins of yours?"

Again, Greta shrugged, "What time is Frenzied Biscuit coming to pick you up? He is coming to pick you up, isn't he?"

"His name is Furious Crumpet. And yes he is. Any minute now, in fact."

"Where is he taking you?"

A gentle tap-tap-tapping on the glass door alerted them to the man waiting out in the snow. The sun had long gone down, and his arrival made both ladies jump. Sylvia hurried to unlock the door and let him in.

Furious Crumpet moved with slow, deliberate grace, like a dancer. He held a gloved hand out to Sylvia, and bowed his head, "*Incatanti.*" He said, with no hint of an Italian accent, Greta noted.

Sylvia blushed through her layers of makeup, and batted her eyelashes, "Oh, how charming." She giggled like a schoolgirl.

"You better be good and kind to my Sylv." Greta wagged a finger at the rakish man. Was he in his forties, or thirties even? It was very hard to tell.

"Naturally." Said Furious Crumpet, "And I'll have her home before midnight." He winked.

"And where are we going?" Sylvia asked, gazing up at him with glittering eyes.

"To Ronnies, on St Anne's Square." Crumpet said, linking his arm with Sylvia's, "Shall we?"

He guided her from the Toy Hospital, without her once taking her eyes off him. Greta scowled. He had a funny effect on her friend. It was a strange intoxicating power that Greta did not trust. She watched them stroll leisurely away down the road through the frosty window. As they moved out of sight, she made a decision. Just because she had relented, and allowed Sylvia to make her own mistakes didn't mean that she shouldn't be keeping a friendly eye. Greta grabbed her coat and plastic rain bonnet, threw them on, and left the Toy Hospital, returning briefly to snatch up her loathed but necessary walking stick.

*

Ronnies was bustling with diners, with waiters gliding from table to table carrying drinks and food on black trays, as Greta hurried in under the red awning. It seemed that the strangely increasing snow level was not putting people off venturing out for a meal.

"I'm just having a couple of sherries. Keeping out of the cold." She said to the Maitre D, "Can I perch at this here little table?" The table in question had a good view down the restaurant, despite being tucked awkwardly into a corner by the bar.

"Wouldn't you prefer a more comfortable seat?" The Maitre D indicated a leather arm chair.

Greta shook her head, and placed herself at the table she wanted, "This will do just fine, thank you young man." Here she had a good view through the tasteful elephant-tusk archway and into the wood panelled space beyond. Light from strategically placed candles flickered warmly on cut-glass tumblers of whisky and glasses of chardonnay. Sylvia and her swarthy gentleman sat at a table half way down the restaurant, and were examining their menus.

"Bet he eats like a slob." Greta muttered to herself.

"Beg your pardon?" The Maitre D asked.

"Nothing, lovie." Greta pulled off her rain bonnet and coat, "Actually, can I have a look at the menu? And a sherry."

The sherry and the menu arrived quickly. Greta thanked the waiter and sipped her drink. It was very good. She smacked her lips approvingly. The menu she kept raised to hide her face, and she strained to earwig on her friend's conversation. The chatter of various couples, families, and friend's conversations muddled together, snatching away words and phrases and swapping them all about, until Greta had no idea who was saying what.

She watched her friend and her well-groomed date chat and gossip. Sylvia giggled at his jokes, and he smiled warmly at her with those deep dark eyes of his. He was every inch a gentleman.

Warmed by candlelight and sherry, Greta's mind began to drift, as it was wont to do. So often she dwelt on the terrible years of her life, that she forced her thoughts back to happy times; To when Pevril would take her out on dates, and pick small bunches of flowers for her. He picked them from their neighbour's gardens, as he was too cheap to buy a nice bunch. But times were tough back then, and the gesture was romantic, and made Greta smile. He was a kind man, once upon a time. Greta smiled to herself as she drifted into a sherry-laced reverie. His handsome face smiled down at her, his big doe eyes reflecting her own.

"Be careful." Said the Pevril in her memories. But it wasn't a memory. He hadn't said that to her, not like that, not then. It broke Greta out of her day dream.

"What am I doing?" She said to herself, placing her fourth - or was it her fifth? - glass of sherry down onto the table, unfinished.

"Taking a very long time to decide what to eat." Said a waiter at her shoulder.

Greta shooed him away, and dropped the menu. She was being a suspicious old busybody, and letting her own fears interfere with her friend's happiness. That just wouldn't do. Sylvia was her best friend in the world, and she wanted her to be happy, whatever that meant for them and the Hospital.

Tutting at herself, she pulled on her raincoat and bonnet, and stood to leave. As she did so, something caught her eye that made her pause. It was a trick of the light, or the sherry making her eyes play games with her. For a moment, for the briefest of moments, in the flickering candlelight, it looked very much like Crumpet had horns. But that was silly. People don't have horns. Greta blinked, and the illusion was gone. Leaving some notes on the table to cover her tab, she hurried home.

*

The evening chill got into her bones, and by the time she reached the Hospital's front door, her teeth were chattering and her knuckles were blue. She fumbled the key into the lock and threw herself inside. Shaking off her coat and bonnet, she chastised herself. She was afraid. But of what? Some odd feeling had come over her as she left the restaurant, making her shuffle a little faster, and making her check over her shoulder every few minutes. Was it Crumpet's momentary horns, or Pevril's peculiar deviation from her memory that gave her the willies?

"You're being a daft old biddy." She said, taking a deep, slow breath.

In the silence that followed, something creaked. She gripped her walking stick with both hands.

A creak or a groan in the Hospital was not uncommon. It was a building in need of some attention, and so liable to make noises from time to time. But Greta's nerves jangled. In the darkness of the Toy Hospital, the piles of cuddly and smiling dollies and teddies were sinister.

Glass eyes peered nastily in her direction, watching, waiting.

Creak.

It came from the cupboard.

Half way down the Hospital stood the cupboard that had housed the Christmas decorations, and in which were stored the spare limbs, bags of stuffing, plastic noses, pots of paints, and other such things as they might need in their everyday repair work. It was open. It hadn't been open when she left, had it? The edge of it could be made out in the yellowish light that filtered in from the street outside. Greta edged forward, holding her stick up defensively. Why was it open?

The light switches were by the counter at the rear of the shop. In the sepia-tinged darkness, Greta shuffled around the islands of toys until she could reach the switches, and pressed them all. The lights flickered into life, as did the Christmas fairy lights. The Hospital was a sudden blaze of colour, which startled the old tom cat, who ran out of the cupboard hissing. He shot past Greta, through the kitchen, and up the stairs.

Greta cursed the cat for giving her a fright, very loudly, and with very coarse language, banging her stick on the ground to punctuate her displeasure.

"What was I even worrying about?" Greta tutted to herself, "Damn cat giving me the heebie jeebies!"

She moved to close the cupboard door, but didn't.

"That's why you were in here?" She called over her shoulder to the cat, who hissed from somewhere upstairs in reply, "Looking for mice?"

In the back left corner of the cupboard, a crack had appeared in the skirting board. It looked chewed, or clawed maybe.

"I'll set some traps in the morning."

And then Greta Pudding took herself to bed.

4th of December.

Greta did not sleep well. She had bad dreams, but when she woke, the memory of them flickered and vanished. The cat had slept on the foot of her bed, and she kicked at it to get off.

"I don't want your hairs all over my throw!" She waved her hands at the old tom, who stretched and blinked his one good eye at her, before casually slipping from her bed.

She dragged herself out from under the covers, and into her fluffy dressing gown and slippers, "Sylv?" She called, as she wandered along the little hall and down the stairs, "I'm putting the kettle on. Fancy a spot of tea?" She hadn't heard her come home.

"That'd be magic, thanks love!" Sylvia replied from the other side of her bedroom door.

Ten minutes later they were sat up in their little living room above the Hospital, with the electric fire blazing, and a cup of tea each. Pevril hung silent and still in his birdcage prison.

"So," Greta probed, "How was your date with Frenzied Cracker?"

"Are you ever going to get his name right?"

"Not if I can help it."

Sylvia tutted playfully, "It was really nice."

"Is that it? Come on, tell me all about it."

"There's not much to tell, really. We had dinner, we chatted, and he walked me home." Sylvia smiled happily.

"What did you talk about? Did you find out much about him?" Greta slurped her tea.

"We talked about..." Sylvia paused for a moment, and a frown flickered over her face, "We talked about mundane stuff, you know. Just chit-chat."

"Did he tell you much about Italy?"

"Why would he mention Italy?"

"I thought that was where he was from? That's what he said, isn't it?"

Greta realised she was being a busybody again, but couldn't help herself. There was something about that man that irked her, deep down in her gut.

"He's a very charming man, and we're going out again next weekend. He's properly wining and dining me. It's ever so nice; being wooed like a young lady again. I feel half my age!"

Someone rattled the letterbox of the Hospital, and called their names from the street. Sylvia peered through the window, but couldn't see much due to the frost.

"Who is it?" Greta asked, "We're not open yet. Tell them we're not open yet."

"We're not open yet!" Sylvia mouthed through the window, "I don't think they care."

Grumbling, Greta put down her cup and shuffled away to discover who it was that dared to interrupt her morning brew.

*

"Good morning." Said a chipper gentleman as Greta opened the door. He strolled past her into the Hospital, taking off his bowler hat. He was well prepared for the weather, done up in a duffel coat over a very smart suit.

"Yes?" She asked, "Can I help you with anything? We're not open yet." Despite being a wizard at fixing beloved toys, she had never truly got the hang of 'customer service'. The general public were an inconvenience, and she usually pushed Sylvia forward at moments like this. But

Sylvia was upstairs still, so Greta put on her best smile, which made the man recoil slightly.

At his back, a pale slip of a girl wavered on the doorstep. She wasn't dressed as warmly as the man, yet seemed not to notice the cold. She carried a large wooden box.

"Come in, if you're coming." Greta said, and shuffled her slippered feet to the counter at the rear of the Hospital.

"Ms Pudding, I assume?" The man said, holding out a card.

Greta took and briefly scanned it. She cocked an eyebrow at the man whose name, according to the card, was Gildroy Silver.

"You work for a funeral home?" She asked sceptically, "If you're touting for business you're plum out of luck. Got my affairs in order already." The business card said 'The Funeral Home For The Unusually Deceased'.

"Is Miss Garland about? We have something to bequeath to her." Said Mr Silver.

"Bequeath?" Greta repeated, then called over her shoulder, "Sylv, these visitors are for you."

After a minute, Sylvia appeared behind her business partner, a curious look on her plump face.

"Hallo, love?" She said curiously, "Anything the matter?"

"I am Gildroy Silver, this is my assistant, Miss Moss." The girl nodded a curt hello, then turned her attention to scanning the shelves of the Toy Hospital. "As per the last will and testament of your cousin, Angelica Tiffin, a selection of artefacts have been left to your care."

Sylvia was dumbfounded, "What?" She exchanged a curious glance with Greta, "I've not spoken to Angelica for years! Not since we were teenagers. Why's she leaving me anything?"

Miss Moss stepped forward and placed the wooden box on the counter top. It was an old chest, with art deco metal trim at its corners and adorning its latches.

"How did she die?" Greta asked, with her customary lack of tact.

"Surprisingly, the usual way." Gildroy said.

Greta cocked her eyebrow again, and began to examine this man anew. He wasn't... usual. His eyes were too blue, and his skin too white. As she peered at him, she thought he looked to gleam the way frost does at dawn. He looked as if he was made of snowflakes. She shook her head, telling herself to stop being so silly.

"She died of old age." Miss Moss said. The girl had a similar complexion to Gildroy, and Greta wondered if they were kin. "Sign here, as proof of receipt."

Sylvia signed the slip of paper, and in a flurry the two odd people were gone, leaving the chest behind, looming darkly at them from the countertop.

"So who was it died?" Greta asked, to break the silence that followed the departure.

Sylvia scratched her chins, worry creasing her brow, "The black sheep of the family." She said.

"I thought that was you?"

"My family has a flock."

Greta nodded at the box, "So open it then."

Sylvia reached out and took hold of the lid, then paused, and looked at Greta with a sudden intensity, "Did you ever wonder why I believed you, right from the off, about Pevril's ghost?"

Greta returned her friend's odd look, "Because you're not daft. You know I'm not daft, either. I told you I was being haunted, and I was."

"No one else would have believed so readily. Ghosts? Pfft! Fantasy and the product of a vivid imagination, folk'd say. Angelica Tiffin, well, she was a witch." Sylvia paused there to gauge Greta's reaction before she ploughed on, "I didn't really keep up with her side of the family, but whispers spread, as they will do. And I started hearing things about her, from very reliable sorts, about... uncanny abilities. She had quite a career, dabbling in spooky gubbins, and Spiritualist sort of affairs. From what I heard... she could talk to the dead."

Now Greta reacted. She slapped the counter top with her palm, "Perfectly timed, then, isn't it? Her carking it?" She said sarcastically.

"It is?"

"Perfectly timed to be of the least help. Why didn't you mention her before? Could have come in handy with all the nursery rhyme palaver I've had to endure over the last few years!"

"Truth be told, I'd forgotten all about her." Sylvia admitted, ashamedly, "Hadn't spoken since we were kids, never attended the same family gatherings. It was only through a friend of a friend of a friend that I ever kept up to date with where she lived, and what she was up to. And that was always vague as all hell, anyway."

"Mm-hmm." Greta eyed the chest, "Yet she left you this box, and some 'artefacts'. Best not be anything sinister! If I find a ouija board in there, it's going straight in the bin."

"I'm rather surprised, honestly, I thought she had died years back. She must have almost been a hundred years old!"

Greta prodded the box, "So open it."

"But it might be witchy paraphernalia."

"All the more reason to crack it open and take a peek!"

Sylvia sucked her cheek, thinking.

Huffing, Greta grabbed a hold of the box and yanked the lid open, "You daft old thing." She said.

Sylvia garbled out a few mashed syllables of panic as the lid fell back, but nothing untoward occurred. She had been terribly worried that the box was somehow booby trapped by a curse, or a spell, or some impish mischief.

It was just a dusty box.

The two old women peered in, mystified by the bright pink fabric contained in that ominous casket.

"Velvet." Greta said, rubbing it between her thumb and forefinger, "Pink velvet?"

Sylvia rolled up her sleeves, and dug her hands into the box. Bound up in the aged fabric were a series of full and tatty notebooks, a pack of tarot cards, and right at the bottom, wrapped in several more layers of pink fabric, a small looking-glass. It had a mother-of-pearl inlaid back and handle, and the mirror was pitted, scratched and foggy. Dangling from it was a hand-written note on a string. It said 'in case of emergency, break glass'.

Chapter Three
Little Miss Molly Radish

Greta slapped the tatty notebook shut.

"This is impenetrable!"

The two of them, washed, dressed, and ready for the day, were sat at the Hospital counter examining the contents of the mysterious casket. The notebooks were of varying sizes and qualities, yet all contained the minute and unintelligible handwriting of Sylvia's distant cousin, Angelica Tiffin.

Sylvia put down the magnifying glass she was using to read the notebook in her own hand, which smelled strongly of flowery incense, "I keep telling you, you need varifocals."

"Oh shush. These spectacles have done me just fine for the last ten years, they'll do for ten more." Greta took off her glasses, huffed on them, and gave them an aggressive clean on the sleeve of her cardigan, "What do you make of it, then? All this witchy-woo stuff?"

Sylvia shrugged, "I think they're diary entries, all mixed up with recipes, and astrological zodiac stuff. You know like in the papers, you can see what Mercury has is store for you if you're a Libra, and all that?"

"I don't believe in that hocum."

"But we know ghosts are real. Why not witches? And why not horoscopes?"

"I never said I didn't believe witches weren't real." Greta wagged a finger, "It's just I like to have evidence. Proof. Something that can't be explained away with a little rational thought."

"There were a whole mess of entries about a duck pond, but I can't make head nor tail of what she's on about. Must be written in code or something." Sylvia lifted the magnifying glass once more, and squinted through it, constantly adjusting its distance from the page as she read, "Half of it is boring everyday goings on, and the other half is nonsense, mumbo jumbo, and spooky shenanigans. Listen to this bit 'The mirror circle did not summon the Dear Departed boy as intended. Instead, a great swarm of children were conjured. Likely those that died in the mills of the city. Why they came, I do not yet understand'."

"Eerie." Greta said.

"It's notes from a seance she did sometime in the twenties, here in Manchester!"

Greta looked over the stack of notebooks, the tarot cards, and the mirror, "So why you?"

"Why me what?"

"Why has all this been bequeathed unto you?"

Sylvia shrugged, "I don't know. Unless I'm a witch too?"

"No."

"You don't think so?"

"I'd have noticed by now." Greta said, matter of fact, "I'm very observant."

"Yes, I suppose. Plus, I don't think I'd do at all well with all that eye of newt, tail of cat, knee of eagle stuff. Imagine the smell that'd waft out of the larder! Doesn't bear thinking about."

"I always imagined all those peculiar ingredients were pickled, myself."

"Pickled frog's toes? Imagine getting mixed up and putting them in your dinner when you wanted a bit of gherkin!"

The two of them chuckled, the tension brought with the casket finally dispelled.

"Let's pack all this away, shall we?" Greta said, scooping up the notebooks, "I can't imagine why she'd leave them to you, but I doubt it's anything pressing."

Sylvia nodded, "I'll go put them away in my room."

The items were loaded back into the pink velvet interior of the casket, and Sylvia bundled them away.

Creak.

Greta's head snapped up at the sound. The cupboard door swung gently open.

"Is that you, you mangy moggy?" Greta grumbled, yet peered cautiously over the counter at the open door, without moving from her seat. The cat was not there, "Damn mice."

Greta ground her dentures together as she dismounted the stool, and hobbled to the cupboard. She peered inside at the gnawed hole in the skirting. It looked a little bigger today. Muttering and grumbling, she set to work laying traps across the cupboard floor. Lots of traps.

Greta meant business. When she was happy with the coverage, and satisfied that no little beasties could get across the cupboard without tripping at least five traps, she closed the door.

"That'll sort you little pests right out." She grinned grimly.

For the rest of the morning, Greta worked on the rocking horse's finishing touches. When it was done, she tied a bow around its neck, and stashed it away under the counter. She checked a clipboard, and ticked off a couple of jobs. Next up was a teddy. She found his numbered box under the counter, and started work. In no time at all he was plump, stitched, scrubbed, and had a brand new ear attached.

"Good as new." Greta smiled.

She really did love her work. All these forgotten, mistreated, play-ravaged toys that had once brought so much joy, would do so again. She gave them a new lease of life. She looked at her own knobbly fingers, flexing their aching joints. 'If only someone could do the same for me,' she thought. The teddy was given a bow around its neck, and packed away carefully into its box again. Next was a Puffalump, stained by what looked like red wine.

"Oh dear oh dear." Greta tutted, "That's going to be a bother to get out." She fingered the silky toy, and pondered which of her home-made cleaning solutions would do the trick, without dissolving the delicate fabric.

Greta Pudding had very little affection to spare on human beings, as it all went on the poor unfortunate toys who came into her care, whether through wear or tear or stain. She gave a little bit of her love to each and every one.

"Toys store up the love you give them." She often said to children, when they came with parents or aunts to drop off their beloved playthings for repair, "And then they're like a happy little radiator, giving off love to everyone nearby. That's the magic of toys. And that's what love is, a kind of magic." And she almost believed it.

"You're so good with children, but awful with everyone else." Sylvia once said to her.

"Well everyone else is awful." Greta responded tartly, "But children haven't learned to be awful yet, mostly."

*

Bedtime for Greta arrived with a cup of cocoa.

"You've been at it all day." Sylvia said, sipping her own cocoa, which she had slipped a shot of coconut rum into.

Greta had hardly noticed her friend bustling about serving the few customers that had ventured into the Hospital that day, and accepted the cup of steaming chocolate gratefully.

"I'll be done soon." Greta said, tapping the deflated space hopper that lay across the counter, "Hand me that puncture repair kit.

"Finish it in the morning." Sylvia said, "Drink your cocoa, and get up them stairs. You look drained."

Greta rubbed her eyes. She was very tired, "You're right. This can wait."

"We've been closed for hours. I was wondering what you were up to down here. You missed a right good episode of Brookside."

"Did they find someone else buried under a patio?"

Sylvia switched off the Hospital lights, and the two old women made their way upstairs.

"I'm just going to sit up for a while." Greta said, "I'll pop the radio on nice and quiet so I don't disturb you."

"Do what you like," Sylvia grinned, "I'll be out like a light."

Shuffling her bum into the squishy armchair, Greta breathed in the rich chocolaty aroma of her cocoa. Through the steam, she saw that the cloth over Pevril's cage had shifted slightly, and he was sat watching her. She turned on the radio, and a dreamy piano wafted fuzzily from Classic FM.

"You can stare all you like, there's no chance of you offing this tough old bird." She scowled, "Not while you're doing bird." She chuckled, "After so many years of feeling trapped by you... it's sort of nice to have the tables turned. How do you like it, hmm?" She sighed, and sipped her drink, "Why,

Pev? Come on, you owe me an explanation." The tin solider's head squeaked slightly as it rotated to face away from her. "Why are you still here?"

She had seen those ghost hunting shows on ITV, she knew that ghosts always hung about because of some unfinished business or other. Not minor stuff like they forgot to do some laundry, or didn't quite get to the end of the latest edition of Housewives Weekly. No, it was always profound, grim, and tragic.

"You haunted me with nursery rhymes, trying to kill me year after year." She clutched the warm cup tightly, "Why?"

The piano vanished from the radio, replaced by loud fizzing. Greta turned and whacked the little device, "Blasted thing. Can never get a good signal."

Pevril's tin head slid back around to stare at her. As Greta's attention returned to the ghost of her ex-husband the atmosphere contracted, like the little soldier was pulling the light and warmth of the room to him. The radio popped and crackled, stuttering out broken fragments of music and words. The darkness grew darker, all colour muted, and then Pevril blew a raspberry at her! The room returned to normal, and the tin soldier seemed to lose its agency.

Chopin's delicate tinkling piano picked up where it had left off.

Greta's eyebrows were raised, "You what!" She stood up and marched to the birdcage, grabbing it in both hands and shaking it. The tin soldier fell over and rattled about, seemingly lifeless. Leaving go of the cage, she stood back, and took a deep breath. She was furious. Livid! But letting him tease her and rile her up wouldn't do. She needed a good night's sleep, so she adjusted the cloth of the cage to cover him. It was daft to get so angry over a raspberry. She knew it was. But she needed answers. Pondering supernatural unknowables, she finished her cocoa and took herself to bed.

*

She had bad dreams.

Greta woke in the middle of the night, sitting bolt upright as the memory of the nightmare began to fade. In the nonsense world of the dream, she had been watched by glass eyes surrounded by long lashes, stubby ceramic hands had reached out to grab her, and curly red hair wound around everything like flaming brambles. There was a small, bright smile, somehow sinister in the dark of night, as it drew closer and closer, and closer, opening wide, and Greta fell in...

"Must've been something funny in that cocoa." She muttered, distractedly, fidgeting in her bed. She had dreamed about one of her own childhood toys. A precious, beloved dolly. A lost dolly. One that she hadn't thought about in a very, very, very long time.
The lingering taste of the nightmare faded, and Greta rubbed her eyes. She plumped up her pillows, and nestled back beneath the covers.

"Why am I dreaming about my old dolly?" She muttered to herself, as her heavy eyelids shuttered her against the night.

5th of December.
Somehow the snow was deeper today, once again, than it had been the night before. Intrepid men from the council had been around first thing

with plastic shovels and bags of salty grit, trying to clear the roads. All they had managed to do was churn up the pristine white snow into freezing, dirty slush.

At midday, Furious Crumpet strode through the Hospital, a grin fixed to one side of his mouth. He had somehow avoided getting himself muckied by the slush on the pavement outside. Greta made a sound in the back of her throat, something halfway between a growl and a sigh, and she turned away from him.

Sylvia emerged from the kitchen, beaming. She had heard the door go, and came out with her best customer-ready smile; all eye wrinkles and pink cheeks. As soon as she saw who it was that had entered the Hospital she paused, and glanced, alarmed, at Greta. But Greta busied herself with a box of assorted pins and nails, averting her attention.

"Hello!" Sylvia said, "What are you doing here? We're not due to meet again until the weekend are we? Did I forget? I'm not ready to go out anywhere." Flustered, she waved her hands at her face. She hated being caught unawares, and felt ever so frumpy in her oversized tabard and comfy shoes.

Taking hold of her hands, Crumpet gazed into her eyes, and she seemed to lose herself in that moment. She calmed instantly, in that starry-eyed connection.

"I simply couldn't wait to see you." He said.

Greta listened to his voice closely. There was definitely no trace of an Italian accent. Not even an English accent. His voice was somehow absent of any hints as to its origin.

Sylvia batted her eyelashes at him.

"I hope you don't think it presumptuous, but I have brought you a gift." He produced a present wrapped in shiny silver paper, and tied with a red bow.

"It's a bit early for a Christmas present just yet." She said.

He shook his head, "It's for now, not for Christmas. Open it."

Sylvia took the present, fingering the bow, "What is it?"

"Open it." Crumpet encouraged.

Greta watched as the wrapping and bow vanished under Sylvia's eager fingers, revealing... she wasn't sure what.

"Oh... thank you?" Sylvia said, turning it this way and that, "What is it?"

The object was a cube, made of brass, and appeared to be some kind of clockwork mechanism, judging by what could be seen through one cut-out panel.

"It is a puzzle." Crumpet said, "A toy. I thought you might like such a thing." He was still smiling that half-smile of his. Greta scowled at that smug expression. She shook her head, and turned away, then did a double-take. In the smooth brass of the odd gift, Furious Crumpet's reflection had horns! Greta looked up at the man, and at his little reflection, and up at the man, and back at the reflection. The illusion - if that's what it was - was unmistakable. He turned to her, raising an eyebrow.

"Are you well, Greta Pudding?" He enquired casually.

"Fit as a fiddle." She grunted at him. When she looked back at the brass cube, his reflection no longer had horns, "Though I might need to get my eyes tested."

"I shall not keep you from your work." He said, nodding a curt bow to Greta, before turning to Sylvia, leaning in, and gently giving her a peck on the cheek. The smitten woman held her hand to the kiss as her fancy man departed, as if by covering it she might make it last that much longer, "He's radiant." She murmured.

"You what?" Greta said, taken aback.

Sylvia blinked a few times, as if waking up from a daydream, and looked down at the brass thing in her hand, "What do I do with this?"

"Looks like a fancy paper weight to me." Greta said, picking up and waving her empty mug at Sylvia, "Pop that kettle on, would you?"

Sylvia did, and then took the odd gift upstairs to her room. She put it on the top of the mysterious casket, on the chair by the window, "I'm collecting such odd ephemera." She shook her head, almost amusedly, before closing the door and heading back downstairs.

6th of December.

Greta woke early in the morning, as she once more fell into the grinning mouth of her childhood dolly. Tutting at herself, she clambered out of bed, and made her way downstairs to the kitchen. A cup of tea with honey and lemon would help to purge her of the strange dream.

As the kettle bubbled and spat, Greta noticed the cupboard door edge slowly open once more. The noise of the kettle hid the creak of its hinges. Grumbling about rodents and cursing the business next door for being the ones to let the infestation get out of hand in the first place, she moved to slam the cupboard door shut. The traps had all snapped closed, but caught nothing, and the hole in the skirting was bigger, once again. Clawed, or gnawed, scraped by sharp little points that left a thousand tiny gashes in the soft grain of the wood.

Instead of slamming the cupboard door closed as intended, she descended noisily to ground level. Her hips and knees clicked and clunked loudly in protest. She leaned forward, pushing the tripped traps away, and peered into the crack. There was something in there. Not a mouse or a rat. Something else. But she couldn't make it out.

The kettle clicked off, as Greta peered closer and closer into the hole. Something in the crack peered back at her with blue eyes, and Greta gasped loudly in surprise.

"Sylvia!" She shouted, "Get down here!"

*

"Look in that hole!" Greta pointed rigidly into the cupboard, as Sylvia's confused face appeared from the kitchen.

"What hole? Have we mice?" Sylvia wiped her hands on her tabard, and followed the direction of Greta's pointed finger, "Oh heck." She tutted, "We should put some poison down."

"Look in the hole." Greta said, near enough pushing Sylvia into the cupboard.

"Keep your hair on, lovey! Deary me." Sylvia said as she crouched down, peering into the dark gap in the skirting, "There's something in there."

"I know that!" Greta spat, "What is it?"

"I think it's..." Sylvia squatted lower, "Wait a minute!" She chuckled, straightening up, and grabbed a saw and claw hammer from one of the shelves.

"What are you going to do with them?" Greta backed away from Sylvia's ample rump, as she bent double and folded herself into the cupboard. With gusto, Sylvia Garland went to work on the skirting, sawing a bit, then pulling at it with the claw hammer, then sawing a bit more. With a splintering tear it came away, revealing the true width of the hole in the wall. It was a deep and dark hole, into which something was bundled.

Greta tried to peer over Sylvia's shoulder, but in the confines of the cupboard, could see only the back of her friend's head bobbing to and fro. Sylvia tugged at the thing in the wall, and it came loose, rolled out and unfolded stiffly, staring up unblinking. She picked it up and stood, turned, and held it out to Greta.

"It's a dolly."

Greta shook her head, "This is ridiculous!" Usually she wasn't one to let anything phase her. She prided herself on her rational and pragmatic approach to life. But over the last few days a very ill feeling had been creeping upon her. A strange foreboding. And alongside the bad dreams, the appearance of this dolly gave her pause for alarm. She reached out and took the doll from Sylvia's hands. It was dusty and dirty, scratched, and its hair was a matted clump. The clothes were torn and stained brown.

"Funny thing, last night I had a dream about a childhood toy. A dolly." Greta said.

"A dolly?"

"Molly the dolly. I took her everywhere with me when I was a tiddler. But I lost her. Vanished. I was devastated." The glass eyes of the doll stared blankly forward. "Just like this one."

"Looks like she's been through the wars."

"Do me a favour? Lift up her skirt?" Greta thrust the doll back into Sylvia's hands.

"Do what?"

"Just do it."

Sylvia flipped the dolly over and pulled up her skirt. There, smudged and faded was a series of pen lines, "There's something there. Some writing. Can't work out what it's supposed to say though."

"I'll save you the bother of deciphering it." Greta bit her lip, "It says Greta. This is my Molly. My dolly Molly. Little Miss Molly Radish. Somehow she's come back to me!"

At any other time, the return of Greta's beloved, long lost dolly would have been a joyous reunion. But in her current state of mind, she saw it as more an ominous occurrence than anything worth celebrating.

"It's some kind of Christmas miracle." Sylvia chuckled, "I bet you could fix her up, good as new, in a jiffy!"

"How did she get in the wall?" Greta scratched her head.

"Who can say?" Sylvia shrugged, and closed the cupboard, not bothering to clean up the splintered skirting, "But she's out of there now, and back with her rightful owner."

Greta took and held the scuffed old dolly and glared at it.

*

"I'm seeing menace in my own shadow." Greta chided herself, "It's my imagination getting carried away with itself." She sat at the counter, carefully removing Molly Radish's clothes. She spoke to the doll, and in doing so was speaking to herself, "Bad dreams, and that blasted Pevril, being a stubborn old so-and-so. And a man with horns like a pernicious Satyr coming to steal away my Sylv..." She trailed off as her friend came through carrying two mugs of tea.

"Did you know I was right behind you?" She smiled at Greta, who took the brew gratefully, "And you have nothing to worry about."

"Why would I worry about anything. I've not a concern in the world." Greta sniped.

"I'm not going to be stolen away like in some Greek or Roman myth. I'm not going anywhere. I like it here, living with you, working in the Hospital. It's cosy, it's nice. There's no man on God's green Earth that could replace that." Greta said nothing. "Is that why you've been so off with him?"

"Frantic Conker?"

"Furious Crumpet. You've been thinking I'd up and leave you for a man? You should know me better than that, Greta Pudding." She patted her friend on the back, "I'm not going anywhere."

Greta squeezed Sylvia's hand in thanks, and returned to her work. She wasn't good with sentimental chit chat, so that was that.

She spent several hours with cotton swabs and cleaning chemicals, rubbing down the porcelain limbs and head of the doll, while accessing the best way to clean the body, which was essentially a bag of ancient dry stuffing, possibly wood shavings. She teased out the knots in the hair, and applied moisturising oils. Satisfied with her progress, she left the dolly on the counter, and headed upstairs for an evening in front of the electric fire.

In the evening gloom, the Hospital was an eerie place, and the various muffled sounds of activity from upstairs did nothing to alleviate that strange atmosphere. Something shifted in the shadows, slinking between the toys and around the shelves. The cat. It was stalking something.

Something only it could see. It pounced, but found its claws empty.

Bored of that game, it turned its attention to the dolly on the counter. It slipped up onto the wooden surface silently, and padded across en pointe. It didn't get too close, though. There was something not right. The old tom arched his back and hissed, tail in the air. The dolly did nothing. The cat hissed again, ears flat back against his head. He lashed out with one swift paw, swiping the dolly off the counter. She fell, and landed face-down on the floor. Satisfied, the cat sat back and began grooming himself.

Something went tap-atap-atap in the Hospital, and the cat looked up eagerly. Was that the sound of something new to stalk in the dark? He looked down over the edge of the counter, to where the dolly had fallen. But Miss Molly the dolly had gone. This was not something this feline would notice as peculiar, as it had no concept of animate and inanimate. It only concerned itself with food and not-food, or food-giver and not-food-giver. So it slunk away upstairs, to roll about on the floor in front of the fire.

In the morning, Little Miss Molly Radish was on the counter once again.

7th of December.
The evening gloom descended quickly, freezing the slush of the streets into uneven sheets, over which only the bravest of shoppers ventured to skate. Sylvia had spent a good few hours applying her makeup and selecting an outfit, for tonight was to be her second date with Furious Crumpet!

"You look at him like a schoolgirl. All giddy." Greta needled her friend.

"I'm allowed. I'm a grown woman." Sylvia stuffed her handkerchief up her sleeve, and checked the contents of her handbag for the fifth time, "Mints, keys, purse, screwdriver, tweezers, perfume, needle and thread, spare buttons..."

"You won't need half of that stuff."

"I like to be prepared." She closed her purse, "You really don't like him, do you?"

Greta sighed, deciding it best to be honest, "No."

"Why, Greta? What's not to like about him?" Sylvia seemed hurt.

"I don't know." Greta replied, "And that's the truth. I admit I was worried about a man coming in and sweeping you off your feet, that you might up and leave the Hospital. That you'd leave me all alone. That's true."

"I'm not going anywhere."

"I know, I know. I was being a fretful, paranoid old dafty." Greta shook her head, "But I can't shake the feeling he's after something. I get a very strange feeling when he's about. Something off. Something I don't like, and I can't for the life of me fathom it out."

Sylvia looked at her friend for a long time, "I'm perfectly safe with him." She said.

"I hope so." Greta gave Sylvia a brief flash of a smile, "You know your own business. It's not for me to go busybodying about, getting in the way of romance. Your mistakes are yours to make, and your happiness is yours to find."

Molly the dolly sat on the counter, clean and dressed in new clothes. Greta fingered the stiff hem of her red checked dress.

"I appreciate your worry." Sylvia said, "I know you're only looking out for your old friend; daft old Sylvia Garland. But try not to worry, hmm? Treat yourself to a soak in the bath tonight, read a book. Relax. You've not been sleeping right for a few nights."

"Is it that obvious?" Greta pushed her glasses up her nose.

"You've been making noises in the night. Waking me up."

"I have?"

"Crying out, whimpering. Never lasts very long, so I figured it was just a bad dream. But it's been most nights this week now." Sylvia opened her handbag to check the contents for the sixth time.

Greta scowled, she only remembered having bad dreams over the course of two nights. She wondered what had disturbed her sleep the other nights.

The door opened, and Furious Crumpet stood immaculately presented in the doorway. He always wore a suit and tie, and never the same twice. Always a new suit, in a new cut, with a coloured shirt, matching tie and pocket square. Tonight the ensemble was in shades of green paisley.

"You look exquisite, Miss Garland." He said.

"Oh hush." Sylvia blushed, "And it's high time you called me by my first name."

"As you wish, Sylvia." He bowed slightly, and his eyes locked with hers. They dazzled her, sparkling with a deep, rich mystery. He was like spiced coffee, like an eternity-aged rioja. To Sylvia Garland he was heady and exotic. He was like a drug, that made her bashful and girlish.

Greta watched him closely. He could turn it on and off at will, that charm of his. She didn't trust him.

Sylvia took Crumpet's arm, and they headed out into the evening chill.

"Don't wait up." Crumpet winked at Greta over his shoulder, and then closed the door.

Greta did wait up. She tried reading a book, some latest best-seller or other. But she couldn't concentrate on it. She ran herself a bath, got in, but sat there stewing rather than relaxing. She was out and drying herself on her favourite fluffy towel in less than ten minutes.

Sat in the living room with the fire on, she eventually found her eyelids getting heavy. She could hear Pevril shifting about in his cage, but she let her eyes close, and her breathing grew slow and shallow. Sleep was coming upon her, and no matter how much Pevril thrashed and clanged and bounced angrily about in his cage, she didn't stir. She began to snore.

She woke with a start, and wiped the dribble from her chin. She had been sleeping with her mouth open. Pevril was still. Whatever he had been doing, clattering about, had exhausted him. What had woken her up?

There were voices in the Hospital downstairs. As Greta listened, she identified two individuals.

"Oh." She said, as she realised that Sylvia had invited Crumpet back for coffee.

She checked her watch. It was half past midnight.

Sylvia giggled, and wittered on. Furious Crumpet said very little, and when he did speak it was too low and quiet for Greta to make out. Then they were quiet for a while. Just as Greta began to think they'd gone out again, she heard two sets of footfalls coming up the stairs.

"She never has!" She muttered to herself, "She wouldn't!"

But she had.

Sylvia had invited Furious Crumpet up to her room, to stay the night.

Greta hurried to her own bedroom as soon as the coast was clear. She hoped the distance between their bedrooms would be enough to avoid accidentally listening to anything they got up to. She buried her head under a pillow, and willed herself back to sleep.

The Toy Hospital — Rylan John Cavell

Chapter Four
Bitter Pudding

Pevril sat at the window, in the dark, watching the sky. The air raid sirens hadn't sounded for a year, and the nights no longer held the threat of falling bombs. Manchester twinkled in the dark. The moon back-lit the clouds, casting undulating waves of light that rolled across the rooftops. From their home in Oldham, perched up high on a steep slope, he had a panoramic view.

"Come away and draw the curtains." Greta said, wiping her hands on the apron tied about her waist. She was mucky with flour and eggs from the pie she had been making. The house smelled of fresh pastry and rich gravy, "Dinner will be ready presently." The pie smelled delicious, but would taste the opposite. She was not a very good cook.

"I'm not hungry." Pevril said.

"You're always hungry." Greta moved to his side, and reached to pull the curtains together.

His hands shot out to stop her and he growled, "Leave me be."

Greta snatched her hands back, tutting, "There's no need for that." She scolded him, "There's nothing in that sky to worry about except the rain, and we've anoraks and umbrellas for that."

Her husband didn't look at her, he simply stared at the sky. Watching, waiting. Greta shook her head, and retreated to the kitchen. During the war Pevril had retreated into himself. It had been by tiny increments, so went unnoticed for the longest time. But the war had been over for a year. Victory had been triumphantly declared. True, rationing and the bomb craters persisted, but the pallor of war lifted, and people relaxed their shoulders, unclenched their jaws, and smiled not through necessity, but through happiness. Everyone except Pevril Pudding, that is. He didn't smile any more. He said very little, simply existing in the house alongside Greta. They drifted about and did their chores as if in a dream of marriage.

Greta kept herself busy, as she thought a good wife should. And she started up a little home business. At first she mended coats and collars and cuffs on her old sewing machine. It was a foot pedal operated family heirloom, passed down from her grandmother. She made a few shillings here and there, enough to keep the coal man happy, and get them an illicit additional ration of bacon now and again.

As word spread of her skills at the machine, the pile of clothes to mend grew and grew, until it took over the living room entirely.

One afternoon she was paid a visit by a small boy. He was in tears, and at first she thought to shoo him away from the front step with a broom. The boy held up a toy, a knitted rabbit.

"Please, Miss? Are you the sewing lady?" He said through sniffles, "They pulled off his ear."

Greta could hear the hyena cackles of a gang of young boys further down the street, and took pity on the mite, "Come inside." She said.

She sat him on a chair by the fire, and examined the rabbit, "What's his name?" She asked.

"Hoppy." Said the boy, wiping his nose on his sleeve.

Greta nodded, taking up a needle and thread, "I usually charge for my services." She said, which alarmed the young boy immensely.

"I've not got any money." He reached to take back the bunny.

"But as this is an emergency situation," She said, pushing him back into his chair, "I shall make an exception."

She set to work with the needle and thread, and in only a couple of minutes, surgery was complete, and she held Hoppy up to admire her handiwork, "Good as new."

The boy hugged her tightly, briefly, and cuddled Hoppy to his chest, burying his face in the rabbit's ears.

Word spread even faster amongst the children of Oldham than it did the adults, and soon Greta Pudding found herself mending just as many toys as she was coats and dresses and trousers.

Pevril would watch from his armchair, ostensibly reading the morning's paper, yet in truth mesmerised by his wife's skills at fixing those beloved toys. He even began to feel a little jealous of the attention she gave those stuffed artefacts.

Their button eyes and stitched smiles seemingly mocked him, as Greta's nimble fingers performed little miracles. He watched her smile, as each one was fixed. That smile, that he never saw directed his way any more.

Pevril's left leg, his bad leg, often gave him gyp in the cold, and the heat, and if he was tired, and when he wasn't. He didn't like going anywhere, for fear of being pitied for being lame.

"I'm not to be put out to pasture, not yet." He often grumbled.

They had been relying mostly on his father for money, as the amount Greta could make on her repairs to garments and toys was limited. But their ability to rely on the elder Pudding's money would soon end, for he was very old and ill. And when the inevitable day came that Pevril laid his father to rest, he didn't cry. He stared glassy eyed as the coffin was lowered into the earth, and the Minister spoke empty words.

Though outwardly numb, something in him was stirred by his passing. Something took a hold of him, and for a fortnight he was busy, out of the house, limping about Manchester on various errands.

"Where have you been?" Greta demanded one windy Wednesday evening in spring, "Your tea's been in the oven keeping warm for two hours! The mash'll be dry as dust by now."

Pevril hadn't smiled, but he was enthused. He was more animated than ever before, and lay out several sheets of paper onto the dining table, "I've sold mam and dad's house." He said.

Greta looked at the papers, unsure of what it was she was looking at, "Very nice. Maybe now we can afford a new mattress. That lumpy old thing needs taking around the back and putting out of its misery."

But Pevril wasn't listening, "And I've accepted an offer on our house too..."

"What!" Greta was incensed, "Why didn't you talk to me about that? Where are we going to live?" She paused, scowling, "When did you even have folk over for viewings?"

Pevril shrugged, "You were out."

"You've gone behind my back, Pevril Pudding, skulking about and pulling the rug from under me-"

He interrupted her, "So that we can afford this." He took out a photograph from amongst the papers. It was of a bakery.

Greta snatched the photo and stared at it closely.

"What have you gone and bought a bakery for?"

"It's not a bakery any more. It's empty."

Greta sat heavily at the table, leaning her head on one hand, "I don't follow." She sighed, "What are we going to do with an empty shop?"

"I've been watching you work. You're good." As compliments go, that was high praise indeed from Pevril, and it made Greta sit upright, "So I thought, why not do it properly?"

"I'm not a professional seamstress." Greta said.

"But you could be. And we wouldn't just open a simple tailoring shop, it'd be a tailors for broken toys. Toy repairs."

"A toy hospital?" Greta wasn't sure whether to be flattered by Pevril's perception of her skills, or terrified at the prospect of this new future he had thrown them into.

*

"A what?" Sylvia giggled, hands on hips, staring at the dirty shop front.

"A toy hospital." Greta said again.

They stood on the pavement opposite the building, glaring at the dull red brickwork, and the lopsided old bakery sign.

"And Pev's just gone and bought it? On a whim?" Sylvia sniffed, "How unlike him. He's never been one for whims."

Greta clenched her teeth. It was clear to Sylvia that her friend was worried, so she took her by the arm and pulled her close, "Well who'd have thought it; Greta Radish growing up, getting married, and becoming a businesswoman!"

"Not exactly the future I imagined."

"It never is." Sylvia side-eyed her friend, "Still no luck on the bedroom front?" She probed.

"Oh hush." She tutted, wary of passers by over-hearing a private conversation, "But no." She whispered, "I knew things would slow down after marriage, but, well, someone slammed the breaks on."

"If you need to oil his wheels to get him turning over, let me know. I've a few tricks and tips." Sylvia winked, and Greta giggled, embarrassed.

The front door to the shop opened, and Pevril emerged from the dim interior. His face soured at the sight of Sylvia, "The van's parked in the alley round back. The guys are moving the furniture in for us. You'd better get here and tell them where you want it all going."

The two women made their way across the road, arm in arm. When they reached Pevril, he moved between them, and guided Greta within. She stepped slowly through the doorway, aware suddenly of the smells of damp and dust in the air. Pevril shut the door in Sylvia's face, leaving her on the pavement outside.

"What you doing with that slapper?" He asked, "I've told you to stay away from her. We have to be respectable now. She can't be seen here. She's got a bad reputation."

On the other side of the door, Sylvia tapped on the glass, "I can hear you." She said, "Don't worry Greta, you get yourself sorted and let me know when you're ready. I'll pop by with a housewarming gift for you."

"You'll do no such thing." Pevril growled then took hold of Greta by the elbow and marched her through the shop to where the delivery boys were waiting for instructions, "The furniture isn't going to arrange itself."

Greta pulled her arm free of her husband's grasp, and nursed it gently. He had gripped it very tightly. The young men leaned in the yard at the back of the building, smoking. Pevril stood with folded arms, and Greta turned away from him. It wouldn't do to make a scene in front of hired help.

"Let's get the bedroom furniture in first. Upstairs, at the front, the room on the right, currently wallpapered in green." The delivery men nodded, "Chop chop. The sooner we get it in, the sooner I can make you all a cup of tea."

This was the encouragement they needed, and soon the delivery men were jogging back and forth, twisting and turning furniture into the new Pudding home.

*

The grand opening came and went, and they made ends meat. Greta took classes to learn basic woodwork and metalwork skills, as more and more of the toys that came to them were articulated or structured in unexpected ways. Pevril paid for the lessons to be done at the Hospital, so that Greta didn't have to suffer the unseemly world of the builder, the joiner, or the smith, as Pevril saw it. She learned quickly, and soon had all the skills necessary to undertake any task that presented itself.

Not only did the Hospital take in toys for repair, but they started to take donations of unwanted playthings too, and sometimes to buy old and disfigured toys that found themselves unloved. These were fixed up, washed, and made presentable, then sold to new owners.

Greta began to despise the adults who came into the hospital, treating the toys like things. They were objects of affection, and joy, and comforting friends, and soothers of sorrow, and the driers of tears. Toys were special. She engaged only with the children, leaving Pevril to handle the money and the adults that passed through the Hospital.

*

"I want to redecorate." Greta said one evening, as they sat and ate dinner on their laps in the living room, "We only tarted it up a little when we moved in. Now we've made enough money, we should put some of it back into the place. A new sign, a new carpet. Box off that weird alcove downstairs to make a tool cupboard. I've spoken to a man who paints pub signs about doing something for us."

Pevril jabbed his fork at Greta, dripping a blob of gravy onto the carpet, "You don't talk to anyone without me being there. I handle the money."

Taken aback, Greta clenched her teeth, "I didn't think it would be a problem."

"We don't need to redecorate. The Hospital is fine as it is." Pevril speared a boiled potato, and wiped it around his plate, before stuffing it into his mouth. When Greta went to say something else, he held up a finger and said, "Enough!" Spitting potato crumbs.

"What's got into you?" Greta said, putting aside her plate, dinner half eaten, "You're forever in a foul mood. I'd rather sit alone than with you currently." Pevril ate in silence. "Honestly, I slave away downstairs, while you swan about, relying on me. I'm not a work-horse you know. You could pull your damned weight now and again!"

Pevril threw his plate onto the floor, sending gravy, potatoes and peas in all directions, "Shut the fuck up, woman!" He stood up stiffly, and left the room.

"Clean that mess up!" Greta shouted, after a moment of surprised silence, "Pevril Pudding, what the hell is the matter with you?"

When he didn't reply, she followed him from the room. Her blood pumped hot in her ears. She had quietly put up with her husband's low mood and odd outbursts for so long, that to finally confront him over it sent a dangerous thrill through every nerve.

He limped away from her towards the stairs.

"I'm going out."

"No you're bloody not." She said, gripping his arm, "You're marching your sorry self back into that living room to clean up your mess. Then when you've calmed down you're going to explain to me exactly what's going on!" She folded her arms, "There's something amiss with you, Pevril, and I want to know what!"

"Clear off out of my way." Pevril gave her shove, and turned to move away, but she grabbed at him, lashed out at him, pushing against his chest.

"Don't you dare lay a hand on me!" She cried out, "There's something wrong with you." They struggled there, at the top of the stairs, "You're useless!" Greta spat, "A useless excuse for a husband. You're good for nothing." Her blood whistled like a kettle, her words spilling out sharp and serrated. She wanted to hurt him. She pushed Pevril down the stairs.

He went down like a rag-doll, arms and legs wheeling in all directions as he bounced and slid down the steep steps. He landed on his back, sprawled out on the cold orange tiles of the kitchen floor. Greta had her hands to her mouth, shocked.

"Pev!" She hurried down to him.

"Call an ambulance." He said, wincing, "There's something wrong with my leg."

Greta took a quick look at it. His foot was facing an odd direction. She nodded and snatched up the shop telephone, spinning the dial as fast as it would go; 9 9 9.

"I need an ambulance. It's my husband. He's... fallen down the stairs." Greta stammered down the line.

Pevril Pudding stared at his wife while he awaited the ambulance. He had been a conflicted man. Plagued by a hangover of war, and pitying himself for his injury, he also felt guilt at having survived when so many did not. He was jealous of his wife for the passion she had for mending toys, jealous of the toys she mended, and the love she showed them; love she no longer showed him. Love she no longer showed him due to his own self-pity and guilt forcing him to push her away. He craved her affection, yet felt supremely unworthy of it. All of this boiled and bubbled in his brain, making him angry and resentful of the life he thought would mend their wounds. Resentful of the Hospital, resentful of Greta, and resentful of himself.

*

    Pevril managed to escape with only a broken ankle and a collection of ripe-plum bruises. He was fixed up and back at home before he should have been, and the incident was never mentioned. The Puddings barely spoke for several days, and Pevril set himself up in their spare bedroom, leaving Greta the larger room at the front. She found it galling, that empty bed. That empty space beside her seemed cursed, colder than it should have been, and so she kept to her side, and to the very edge, where the small radiator kept her from shivering at night, swaddled in layers of crocheted blankets.

Greta returned silently to her work, filling the days from first light to late at night with what she loved to do, while spending as little time upstairs as possible. Pevril was different now. He seemed almost to have liberated himself from everything that was holding him back previously, and now the bitterness that had eaten away at the core of his being finished its meal, leaving nothing but the skin of her husband. Inside was someone else. Someone new. Someone vindictive and vile.

One autumn evening, Greta heard an unfamiliar sound. It was coming from upstairs, and at first she struggled to identify what it was. But after a minute of rummaging in her mental catalogue of familiar noises, she realised that Pevril was laughing!

She put down her needle and thread, and the teddy whose paw she was mending, and hurried upstairs. She followed the sound to the living room and found her husband, red cheeked and with tears running down his face, with a book open on his lap. The pages were illustrated with blue and green watercolour doodles, and the text stood large on the page. A children's book.

Greta hadn't heard Pevril laugh in years, and she smiled, beginning to chuckle. His laughter was infectious. Warm memories came flooding back, of their early romance, and how they had laughed and joked, making merry.

"What's so funny?" She asked.

"These nursery rhymes!" He wiped the tears from his eyes, "They're hilarious!"

Greta pulled the book from his lap and read aloud, "Peter, Peter, pumpkin-eater, Had a wife and couldn't keep her; He put her in a pumpkin shell, And there he kept her very well." Her smile fell as she read, "What's so funny about that?"

Pevril waved a hand at Greta, "Imagining you stuffed into a pumpkin, like a big orange corset!"

Greta threw the book down, and tutted.

"What's so funny about that?" She asked again, more angrily.

"Would you like to be stuffed into a pumpkin?" He chuckled, "You're starting to look the shape of one." He prodded her belly with a sharp finger.

"Get off." She batted away his hand, shocked, and feeling suddenly ugly, and left the room. As she stomped down the stairs, she heard him cackling to himself, and shuddered. It wasn't a nice laugh. It was almost manic.

*

Several weeks later, one wet afternoon, Greta went through the kitchen cupboards searching for a snack. She came upon a small red box of raisins. Taking them out, she returned to her work at the Hospital counter. Now and again she plucked a raisin from the box, and chewed it slowly as she worked.

After a while she became aware of Pevril at her side, suppressing a giggle.

She ignored him, and put another raisin in her mouth. He moved around the Hospital, watching her. Finally, she put her hands on the counter top, and glared at him.

"What?" She demanded.

"Don't mind me." He said, a weird little smile on his face.

Perturbed, Greta thought it best to ignore him, and returned to her work. As she did so, Pevril began to quietly sing a nursery rhyme.

"I know an old lady who swallowed a cow, she swallowed the cow to catch the goat, she swallowed the goat to catch the dog, she swallowed the dog to catch the cat, she swallowed the cat to catch the bird, she swallowed the bird to catch the spider that wriggled and jiggled and tickled inside her! She swallowed the spider to catch the fly…"

Greta pulled another raisin from the box, but then paused, and looked up at Pevril, who was no longer giggling. She ripped open the little red box of raisins and poured them over the counter. Amongst them were three dead flies. Open mouthed, she stared at her husband.

"Perhaps she'll die." He said, then stalked away.

Chapter Five
Break Glass Point

8th of December.

"That puzzle box thing has started ticking." Sylvia said, as she waited for the kettle to boil.

"Oh yes?" Greta crossed her arms, and raised an eyebrow.

"Clockwork or something."

"Or something." Greta watched as Sylvia took three cups from the cupboard, "Did he see to your wants and needs?"

Sylvia's cheeks flushed in scarlet embarrassment, and she began to stutter out a string of nonsense syllables, "Well, I, you see, he, we, and then, I thought, the wine, um..." She gave Greta puppy eyes, "Please don't be angry."

Greta shook her head, "I'm not angry, Sylvia Garland. I'm disappointed. I thought your wanton ways were a thing of the past."

Sylvia shrugged, "Can't teach an old dog new tricks."

"Bet you could teach him a thing or two, though." Greta winked, the show of disapproval ended, "Just so long as you're being careful."

"We used protection!"

"I didn't mean that."

"Oh, you mean emotionally?"

Greta nodded.

"I am." Sylvia said, pouring the hot water into the pot, "At least, I'm trying to. But he is slightly marvellous."

"Are you falling for him?" Greta asked.

Sylvia shrugged, "I've not felt this way about a man for a long time. I might be."

Greta nodded, "Well take it slow and steady. Don't let him get too comfortable, or he'll stop being such a gentleman. Such is the way with blokes. As soon as they can stop making an effort, they will. Lazy breed."

Sylvia let Greta rattle on. It wasn't the first time she had heard these remarks, and doubted it would be the last.

"Is he staying for long?" Greta asked, eventually.

"I shouldn't think so. He's got some kind of business meeting today." Sylvia stirred the teabags in the pot.

"What business is he in?" Greta probed.

Pausing distractedly, Sylvia scowled.

"Something to do with an ambassador. Maybe. I can't remember."

"An ambassador?" Greta said, impressed, "The Italian ambassador?"

"Why Italian? You're obsessed with Italy. What's that about?" Sylvia chuckled.

"He said he was Italian, I'm sure he did." Greta began to doubt her memory, "Didn't he? When he first introduced himself?"

"I can't recall." Sylvia poured Greta a cup of tea, then loaded up a tray with the pot, honey and lemon, and the two remaining cups, "Is it important?"

"No I suppose not." Greta shrugged, as Sylvia carried the tea things up the stairs, "I hope not, anyway."

"You going to join us for your morning brew?" Sylvia said, pausing on the stairs.

Greta was about to say something along the lines of 'not on your nelly', but on catching the hopeful look on her friend's face, she changed her mind, "If you insist." She said.

Sylvia smiled, and continued up.

Greta hid her look of disgust when she entered the living room. Crumpet was slouching in her seat! He seemed to be very much at home. Sylvia fussed around him, pouring the tea.

"Lemon and honey?" She asked.

He shook his head, smiling. He then noticed Greta loitering in the doorway, and turned his lighthouse beam of charm upon her, "Good morning, Ms Pudding." He said.

Greta turned away from him, letting that strange gaze of his land on a cold shoulder, moving to peer out of the window. She observed that overnight, unseen clouds had worked at raising the level of slush and ice across Manchester's pavements to dangerous levels.

Crumpet sipped his tea, and nodded at Pevril's shrouded cage in the corner, "You should uncover your bird. The poor thing won't do well in the dark, day and night."

"It's not a bird, it's..." Sylvia stopped herself before saying something she might regret, "It's not a bird." She couldn't think of an explanation, and so changed the subject, "Time's ticking on. Shouldn't you be getting yourself ready and out and about?"

Crumpet nodded, and Greta took note that his attention remained on the cage in the corner. He cocked his head to one side like a dog. He seemed to be listening to something. Greta's ears took a little while to tune in to the sound, and when she heard it her blood ran cold. Pevril was quietly singing.

"Goosey, goosey, gander, where shall I wander? Up stairs, down stairs, and in my lady's chamber. There I met an old man who would not say his prayers, took him by the left leg, and threw him down the stairs."

Crumpet frowned, puzzled, and Greta went pale, "It's an old mechanical bird," She said quickly, speaking loud enough to drown out the tin soldier's voice, "plays ditties, silly little thing, but the internal workings are a bit temperamental. Anything can set it off." She slurped her tea, then nudged the cage, "Hush your noise." She hissed.

Sylvia made to scoop Crumpet up, "Come along then, lovey, it's high time you got yourself up and away."

"You're not kicking me out, are you?" Crumpet play-acted being upset, "I do hope I haven't been too forward."

"You were every inch a gentleman." Sylvia said, blushing, "Now, we have a Hospital to run, and you've..."

"I've places to be, people to see, things to do." He smiled, waving a hand airily, "And all that jazz."

He drained his tea, which was still piping hot, and gave Greta a small bow, "Good luck with fixing your... mechanical bird?" He said, fixing the cage with a curious look.

"A bothersome little thing that should know when to keep its trap shut!" Greta said in Pevril's direction, who was still softly singing the same rhyme again and again.

Crumpet rose and left the room. When she was certain he wasn't lurking within earshot, Greta pulled back Pevril's covering, ready to admonish him with harsh words and a wagged finger. He fell silent as soon as he saw her.

"That's better." She hissed, "I'll have none of your nursery rhyme carry-on, especially while we've other people here."

Pevril's stiff metal face seemed to take on a quizzical expression, as he stared at her with unblinking eyes. Sylvia, biting her nails in the doorway, flustered, muttered, "How are we going to explain a haunted toy soldier to him?"

Greta shook her head and recovered Pevril, "We aren't going to have to explain anything. Pev will keep schtum when we've guests over," She raised her voice pointedly as she said, "If he knows what's good for him."

Sylvia puffed, "But it's not normal. Is it? He'll find out, and he'll run a mile. It'll scare him off me, I just know it."

"Pull yourself together." Greta said, barging past her larger friend, "It's about time we started work and opened up. Come along."

*

Greta was at work, pinning the stitches of a threadbare teddy, when Crumpet eventually drifted downstairs. Sylvia fussed over him as he said his goodbyes, but he didn't immediately leave. He lingered, staring at Molly the dolly, who Greta had perched on the top of the cash register.

"What an interesting toy." He said, "Is it yours?"

Greta nodded, "Yes. It's my childhood dolly."

"We found it in a hole in the wall, weirdly." Sylvia said, "No idea how it got in there."

"Yes." Greta said, giving her friend a firm 'sshh' eyeballing, "Lots of weirdness going on of late."

"It is the season for it." Crumpet stroked his chin, "May I see it?"

"Looking's with your eyes, and you can see her dandy from there." Greta jabbed her well-pricked pin cushion meaningfully, "Have a lovely day." She said.

Knowing that he had been dismissed, Crumpet bowed to Greta, kissed Sylvia on the cheek, and departed.

Greta muttered to herself, "Lots and lots of weirdness going on of late."

Sylvia bustled about the kitchen, making a shopping list, and quite a bit of noise, "I'll pop out and get some essentials." She said, "And maybe do a little scouting for Christmas goodies, while I'm at it."

Distractedly, Greta nodded, and gently ground her dentures. There had been a lot of weirdness going on of late, and Greta didn't like it. She felt as though someone were playing a game with her, and hadn't told her the rules. In a whirl, Sylvia had vanished from the Hospital to carry out her errands. Greta watched her trudge slowly from the front door, fighting against the snow drifts.

"Christmas." Greta muttered to herself, "Christmas." She hadn't yet got a gift for Sylvia, and as with every year, she found it tricky to decide on what to get her.

That's the thing with age - at a certain point you realise you've got almost everything that you want, and Christmas gifts become things you need instead; Thick socks, a new rain bonnet, a fresh pack of handkerchiefs, and so on.

The fun and excitement had long gone out of the season for Greta, though she always tried her damnedest to make it a jolly time of year.

Deciding to begin her yearly bout of festive espionage, Greta made her way up the stairs and to Sylvia's bedroom door. She paused there a moment, her hand on the knob. She mentally crossed her fingers that any signs of the previous night's debauchery had been tidied away. She gripped the knob and let herself into Sylvia's small room. The few items of furniture that there were bulged full of clothes and keepsakes.

Greta started at the window sill, where Sylvia kept her bottles of perfume lined up. She checked each of them to see which would be running out first. They all seemed pretty full. Next she pulled open the dresser drawers, and briefly examined the socks and so on that were jammed in there. It all appeared to be relatively new, and in plentiful supply. As Greta went about the small room, she found nothing that would give her a clue for what to get for Sylvia. She stopped, and scratched the bridge of her nose thoughtfully, listening to the clock tick tick tock tock away the seconds.

Tick tick tock tock? Greta looked at Sylvia's small bedside clock. Was it ticking twice as often as it should? She picked it up and listened. No. It was ticking normally. Placing the timepiece back on the bedside table, she cocked her head, and followed the sound. The extra ticking was coming from Crumpet's puzzle-box thing. She picked it up, and turned it over in her hands, feeling the smooth surfaces, and the hard, cool metal from which it was made. There seemed to be a great many tiny lines, running in spirals and zigzags over its faces. Were they engraved decoration, or openings? Would this thing twist and turn like a Rubik's Cube? She gave it an experimental tug, trying to make it do something. Nothing happened. Shrugging, she put it back. But then her curiosity got the better of her. Maybe Sylvia might like a gift connected to her witchy relative. Perhaps a book of potions and home remedies? That could be a good idea.

She removed the ticking puzzle box from the top of the chest, and lifted the lid. Amongst the pink velvet nestled the notebooks. Flicking through quickly, she decided that there weren't already potion recipes amongst the scribbles, and so that could be the perfect gift idea.

They wouldn't be real magical potions or course, but tinctures for health and home remedies were likely what inspired the ideas of storybook witches and their bubbling cauldrons in the first place.

She picked up the mirror next, and examined it. The hand written label said 'in case of emergencies, break glass', but whatever could that mean? With a twang the puzzle box jumped slightly into the air, as some mechanism inside wound itself up and released. Greta leaped in alarm, and the looking-glass slipped from her hand. It fell in slow motion, as she grabbed ineffectually at it. Landing face down, she didn't see it shatter, but the sound was unmistakable. She closed her eyes, and prayed for a moment that the dreadful sound of breaking glass had been in her imagination, but when she opened her eyes, reached down, and gently picked it up.

As she lifted it, a sudden blast of sickly incense stung her eyes, and the smoke from a recently extinguished candle seemed to drift into the room. It made Greta sneeze. No sooner had these fragrances appeared, they were gone again, and Greta wondered if she hadn't in fact imagined them!

A few thin shards of mirrored glass lay on the floor, and the mirror itself had a spider's web of thin cracks across it, breaking her reflection into thirty-odd disjointed pieces.

"Sylv is going to be miffed at me for this." She said.

"What's the emergency!" Someone demanded at her shoulder, making her jump once again.

Greta spun about, "Who's there?" She was alone.

"This isn't right. Who are you?" Said the voice, and Greta felt a pressure at her shoulder, as if someone laid a hand there, but she was alone.

"Who am I?" Greta spat, "Who are you!? Where are you?!"

"It might help if you look in the mirror." The voice sounded impatient.

Raising the mirror to eye-level, Greta saw her reflection, as well as the reflection of someone else. She was not alone in the broken hand mirror. Stood beside her, resting a china-white hand on her shoulder was a young woman dolled up like a flapper; Acidic-blonde bob, thick mascara and clumped lashes peered from the cracked glass.

"Hello, now, what's the emergency, and where is Sylvia?"

Greta checked again with her own eyes, but she was definitely alone in the room. Yet there this young woman was, clear as day, reflected in the broken mirror.

"I don't have all day." Said the reflected spectre.

"I'm Greta." Said Greta, "Who the devil are you? And what are you doing in Sylvia's mirror?"

"Becoming impatient," The phantasmal flapper sniped, "Where is Sylvia?"

"She's gone shopping." Greta said.

The flapper gave Greta a wide-eyed and frustrated look, "Yes? And?"

A dreadful thought occurred to Greta, "Are you Sylv's cousin? The witch? Angie Triffid?"

"Angelica Tiffin." Said the apparition, rolling her eyes, "Yes, I am she. The great Madame Miasma, to those in the know."

Greta wagged a finger at the mirror, "You better not be trying to put a spell on me! I'll have none of that hexing carry-on in my home!"

Tiffin rolled her eyes, "I'm not going to put a spell on you. Couldn't even if I wanted to. Now, answer me one simple question? What is the emergency?"

"There isn't one." Greta said, not quite sure if she was losing her mind or not, "Not right now anyway."

The reflected flapper tutted, putting her hands on her hips, "This mirror isn't a toy, you know!"

Greta rubbed her eyes, "This is madness."

"What's 'madness' is wasting my time!" Angelica Tiffin sighed.

"You're a witch?" Greta asked, trying to get her brain into gear.

"I was a witch." Tiffin said, "I'm not much of anything now, seeing as I'm dead."

Greta floundered, suddenly overwhelmed, "I have a hundred questions. Maybe you can help!"

Tiffin nodded condescendingly, "I'm sure you do. And maybe I could. But first things first; I have a message for my cousin."

"You can tell me." Greta said, "I'll pass it on."

Tiffin shook her head, her acidic bob swishing stiffly, "No. What are you even doing, going through her possessions? Are you some kind of a snoop?"

"I'm her friend!" Greta snapped, "Her best friend."

"Best friends don't go snooping about in one another's knicker drawers. You're not doing much to persuade me you're trustworthy enough to convey a message to her."

Sighing, Greta admitted the reason for her snooping.

"Why not just ask her what she wants? Surely that would be easier?"

Greta shrugged, "Possibly."

"Look, I've not much time available for these visitations." Tiffin said, "Idle chitchat is so terribly draining, don't you find? The clock is ticking.

Wake me up when Sylvia is home." And then she was gone.

"Hello?" Greta waved the mirror about, "Hello? Come back!" But the phantom flapper had evaporated.

The clock was ticking, and so was the puzzle box. Now that Greta paid it attention once again, she discovered that it had changed shape. Only slightly, but changed it had. The shallow lines had been joints and connections between different oddly shaped segments. These segments had shifted, allowing a small crank handle - like the kind that activates a jack-in-a-box - to emerge from one side. Greta packed the mirror and notebooks away, and put the puzzle box back on top.

"I need a cup of tea." She said.

From the doorway, the one-eyed old tom cat watched her curiously, flicking his tail.

*

Sylvia returned a few hours later, and though Greta wanted to broach the subject of the ghost in the mirror, she couldn't quite get the words out, or steer the conversation in the right direction. Every time she thought she might be able to start onto the topic of the witchy casket, Sylvia turned the conversation around to something else.

"I'm feeling like gammon for Christmas dinner this year, how about you?" She said, and "Crumpet's a vegetarian, you know?" And, "Don't bother getting me anything this year. I've got all I need." And, "I picked up a fancy tin of shortbread. But it's not for now. It's for Christmas." And on and on, until Greta gave up.

Sylvia would find the broken mirror and the ghost of Angelica Tiffin whenever she next had a peek within that pink velvet-stuffed box.

*

15th of December.

To Greta Pudding's delight, the week passed without incident. There were no ghostly visitations, Pevril kept quiet, and Crumpet stayed away.

Customers came to collect their mended playthings, and someone from a local charity shop dropped off a big bag of moth-eaten old cuddly toys that they couldn't shift.

"We were told you'd be able to do something with these tatty things?" The old man said from behind a pair of jam-jar spectacles.

"That we can, and that we shall." Greta said happily, as she rifled through the assorted love-worn toys.

The most exciting thing to happen all week was the cat having a sudden fit of the zoomies around the Hospital, knocking over the Christmas tree, and getting tangled in tinsel.

"I don't know why the mangy old thing doesn't bugger off." Greta said, as she huffed and puffed, fixing the tree and the decorations, "I've tried shooing him out the door numerous times, but he just won't go!"

"Probably because I keep feeding him." Sylvia said, "I've rather taken a shine to the old boy."

Greta rolled her eyes, "I might have known you're to blame for his lingering. What have you been feeding him?"

"Just some kippers."

"Those are my kippers!" Greta wagged a finger, "I wondered where they had been going."

"Clive does love them. I thought there wasn't any harm in sharing." Sylvia cooed at the tomcat, as it slunk around her ankles, purring.

"Clive?"

"Yeah, Clive."

"You named him Clive?"

Sylvia nodded, "Had you named him something else?"

"I usually called him Little Bastard, but not to his face." Greta chuckled, "Well, if he's staying with us, I suppose Clive is as good a name as any. But he's your cat. And buy him his own kippers. Mine are fancy, and he can't keep having them."

The cat leaped up onto the Hospital counter and took a swipe at Molly.

"Clive!" Sylvia tutted, "That's not your toy."

"The little bastard." Greta muttered, checking the dolly over for tears. She was unharmed, "Why'd he do a thing like that?"

Clive the cat waited until Greta had put Molly back in her place, before pouncing, grabbing hold of the dolly's soft belly in his teeth, and racing off with her.

"Oi! Cat!" Greta shouted, pursuing him through the kitchen and up the stairs.

Sylvia was right behind her, "He doesn't mean her any harm. He must think she looks like a cat toy."

Clive the cat dropped Molly as Greta and Sylvia burst into the living room. He darted under the settee and hid, watching with his one good eye. Greta, panting, creaked as she bent down to pick up her childhood toy, and checked her over again for damage.

"You're a bad kitty." Sylvia said, as she reached under the settee to drag the cat out, "Molly Radish isn't your toy!" She man-handled the cat into a bosomy embrace, and pinned him there, cooing at him, "Silly kitty."

"Looks like she's not safe with you about." Greta muttered, "I'll have to keep her somewhere you can't get at her." Her eyes fell upon Pevril's shrouded cage.

She removed the cloth, and unlatched the little door. Pevril's head slid slowly around to look at her, as his prison door began to open. Was this freedom? Was this a chance of escape? No.

Little Miss Molly Radish was stuffed through the small opening, and sat up beside him, blocking his egress. She was considerably larger than him, and filled much of the remaining space. Greta closed and locked the bird cage, satisfied that her dolly was safe, away from the cat.

Pevril stared at Molly Radish with his solder-spot eyes. He didn't appear very happy about his new cell mate.

That evening, Greta and her cocoa went to bed early, leaving Sylvia to watch the latest episodes of her soaps on their fuzzy old television set with Lord Clive McSquinty-Pants - as was his full name - purring happily on her lap. The warm burbling of the tv in the next room sent Greta swiftly off to sleep, buried amongst her many crocheted blankets.

Thud.

Greta woke up in the dark and the silence of the early hours. She shivered, despite her many blankets and the thick duvet. She imagined her breath clouding in the air, it was that cold.

"Has the heating gone off?" Greta murmured sleepily to herself. She silently weighed up her options; stay in bed, and be as warm as she could manage until morning, or dare to brave the winter chill of the Hospital at night to bang the boiler with a spanner until it worked again.

Thud.

The sound had Greta bolt upright in bed, straining her ears.

"What was that?" She wondered aloud.

Thud.

She flung her legs out of bed and jammed her crooked old feet into her fluffy slippers. She grabbed her dressing gown from the back of the door, and hugged it tightly around herself, as she made her way downstairs. Whenever she had been forced to watch a scary film by Sylvia, Greta was always the one to shout at the characters to 'turn on a light', and to not go into the spooky dark place to investigate. Yet here she was going against all her own advice, and marching down the dark stairs towards the thing going thump.

"I bet it's that bloody cat." She hissed.

The Toy Hospital was illuminated in sepia tones by the street lamps on the pavement outside. A square of dirty-yellow light, thrown at an angle by the lopsided window was just enough to see by. In this semi-darkness button-eyes followed her, as she moved around the Hospital. Plastic and porcelain faces stared blankly into the middle-distance, as Greta moved about, trying to discover the source of the sound.

Thud.

She spun around. A wooden nutcracker doll had fallen over, and rocked gently to a stop on the floor. Greta scowled as she picked up the doll, and put it back in its place.

"Clive?" She hissed, "pspspspsps. Here kitty. If you stop this silly game you can have one of my fancy kippers for tea tomorrow."

Something moved amongst the large central table of toys beside her. A dark shape, slinking formlessly from right to left. It was a momentary motion, before becoming still again, but Greta had seen it, and pounced. She pulled apart the piles of toys and found... nothing. No cat.

Thud.

She spun about, her heartbeat quickening slightly, as she saw a stuffed owl launch itself from a shelf. She was certain it would swoop at her, claw her face, gouge out her eyes. But the plush toy with silvery eyes simply bounced on the floor and lay face-down.

Creak-creak. Creak-creak.

Greta was panicking now. All suspicion of the cat being to blame dissolved. Her nerves were frayed, and her dentures chattered in the cold, as a rocking horse in the window had begun to rock by itself. It rocked steadily, without any indication of what made it move.

Creak.

Behind her, the cupboard door eased slowly open, the inside of which seemed darker than it should be, deeper than it was, and hollow.

Greta raced forward and slammed the cupboard shut, shoved the owl back onto its shelf, and forcefully laid her hands on the rocking horse, stilling its motion, "No." She said, "I will not have my Hospital go all peculiar! I will not allow it!"

To whom or what she was speaking, she couldn't imagine, but given all that she had witnessed so far this December, she didn't want to think of the possibilities.

Thud.

Greta ground her dentures together, and looked up. That last thud had come from the living room. As fast she could, she took herself upstairs. Flicking the light switch, she illuminated the room, and squinted in the sudden brightness.

Little Miss Molly Radish lay in the middle of the floor, on her back.

"How on earth…" Greta breathed. Her gaze travelled up to the bird cage, which hung open, and was alarmingly empty, "Pevril Pudding, what have you done?"

16th of December.

Greta didn't sleep. She stayed up all night shivering in her arm chair, hugging Molly Radish for comfort. She wrapped the doll's red curls around her fingers, the way she had done as a child, and fretted.

Yawning, Sylvia ambled into the living room, "What are you doing up already?"

Greta nodded across the room to the open cage, "He's been up to mischief." She said, "Bonking and bashing about in the Hospital all night, scaring me half to death."

Sylvia ran over and examined the cage, "How did he get out?" The little latch was unbroken, and none of the bars appeared bent.

"He's a ghost. Must have mystical ways and means at his disposal."

"But why not use them before now?"

Greta shook her head, "How am I to know that? I'm not a psychic."

Sylvia snapped her fingers, "No, you're not! But we know someone that was! Angelica Tiffin! I bet there's something in her notebooks that can help!"

Greta grumbled, "There's something I should probably tell you."

"About what?"

Rat-a-tat-tat. Someone rapped on the Toy Hospital door.

Sylvia peered out of the window and her eyebrows shot up, "It's that girl. The one who came to bequeath me the box."

Greta scowled, "Now what on Earth does she want so early in the morning?"

Sylvia unlocked the door, and before having said anything, the girl whizzed past her and into the Hospital. She was talking on a mobile telephone and gazing about the place with a most curious expression, "Yes, I'm here now. I'll report back with my initial findings." Said the pale girl.

"Miss Mass, isn't it?" Greta asked from the rear of the Hospital, as the Funeral Home official slid the aerial back into her mobile telephone, and dropped it with a thud into her vast handbag.

"Moss." She nodded her pale head, framed by a raven-black bob, "Do you mind if I ask you some questions?"

Greta aimed a chiding finger across the counter, "If you think I'm signing up for whatever peculiar funerary practices you have on offer, you can turn about and quick-march back the way you came. I'm no witch."

Miss Moss smiled thinly, "Nor did I take you for one."

"And neither am I. At least I don't think I am. Am I a witch?" Sylvia said, almost hopefully.

Miss Moss shook her head, "No."

"Then what do you want?" Greta was feeling particularly impatient.

Miss Moss hefted her handbag onto the counter, and began to rummage about with its noisy contents, "As you may have guessed by the name of the company I work for, we don't deal with humdrum funerals and rites."

"You don't say." Greta folded her arms.

The girl's pale hands pulled from the handbag a pair of binoculars, a telescope, a monocle, a kaleidoscope, and a disposable camera, "I do say."

Greta eyed up the lensed objects littering her counter top, and cocked one puzzled eyebrow, "I repair toys, not stuff like this."

"These are all in working order." Miss Moss proceeded to hold up the telescope to the camera, through which she took a photograph. Then, winding on the film, she took another, facing the other way. Then she swapped to the binoculars, and did the same through each of its four lenses.

Sylvia watched her, thoroughly baffled. The girl did not appear to be looking where she was aiming the shots, "Those are going to come out all blurry. Is this some kind of art project for college?" She asked.

Miss Moss smiled that thin-lipped smile of hers, "No." Pausing, she examined the perplexed and grumpy faces of the old women before her, "Perhaps I should give a small explanation?"

"Perhaps you should." Greta sniped.

"There are some things in this world that cannot be entirely explained. And those things are most often discovered by looking at what's right in front of us with fresh eyes."

Snap, wind wind wind. Snap, wind wind wind.

More and more photos were taken, then she changed to the kaleidoscope, and continued.

"Indeed." Greta said slowly. Wary now, of this slight girl and her peculiar photographs. Perhaps she was aware of the prisoner she had until so recently held upstairs, or of the ghost in the mirror? Was it against some law to keep a ghost prisoner?

"I don't care for your strange attention to my Hospital." Greta said slowly, "So leave, if you'd be so kind. Take your search for ghosts elsewhere."

"Who said anything about ghosts?" Miss Moss shot the old woman a sideways glance that said 'gotcha', "look, you have our card. Anything... untoward... happens, you give us a call."

Greta and Sylvia watched silently as the lensed items were packed away, and the mobile phone retrieved. Miss Moss slid out the aerial, and hit a speed-dial number.

"Mr Silver? Yes. I believe my suspicions will be corroborated, sir." She strolled up the shop, peering at the stacked toys, "I'll get the photos developed right away. See you at the office."

And then she was gone.

"What a strange girl." Sylvia said, "I hope the ones she took of me will come out ok. I tried to give her my good side."

Chapter Six
The Sorry Tale Of The Tin Soldier And The Troll

Listen well, beloved, and I shall tell you the tale of a little soldier made of tin. The man that made him was an old soldier, and made him in his own image; with one damaged leg. The little tin soldier was told by the man that made him, all about his sad life, and his struggles, and his joys, and his wife - long lost to him.

Now, beloved, the tin soldier's head was quite small, and his brains even smaller. So small in fact that he could only manage one and a half thoughts at a time! Not like you and me, with our big, complicated, human minds. The little tin soldier listened to the old soldier, who would often sing children's rhymes to pass the time and amuse himself, though the little tin soldier would not understand them.

When the time came for the old soldier to die, he did so, and left the little tin soldier with nothing but his one and a half thoughts at a time. And it was these one and a half at a time thoughts that got the little soldier into his sorry tale.

There was an old troll, who the tin soldier knew of from the man that made him, who had eaten up the old soldier's wife. She was crooked and ugly, hunched and hairy, and like stars her teeth came out at night. But they did not shine. This old troll lived in a castle, in the dungeon of which she kept prisoner a great many lost travellers, who had the misfortune to call on her for respite on their journeys from near and far. She stuck them with needles - prick prick prick! She bound them in rope - quick quick quick! And she stacked them on shelves - five bodies thick!

It is said that the dungeon was her larder, and the suffering of the travellers made them ever so tasty on her long oily tongue!

Now, beloved, it is true that the little tin soldier was very brave, but due to only being able to have one and a half thoughts at a time, it took him a great long while to decide what to do about this horrid old troll.   He eventually fell upon a plan to kill the old troll woman, and set free the dead soldier's wife from her belly - as well as free the poor unfortunates pricked and bound and stacked in her dungeon.

He posed as a weary traveller, and at her gate she spied him coming along the path with her big yellow eyes. They were as big as dinner-plates, and veined and sour as curdled milk. Now, beloved, wouldn't that make you or I shrink back in fear? Well, the little tin soldier hadn't enough space in his brain for being scared.

'Dear tired traveller, where do you journey to?' Asked the troll woman.

'I come from far, and do go onward far also.' Replied the tin soldier.

'Come and rest a while in front of my fire. I have fine vittles which you may partake in, and which you can fortify yourself with for the journey ahead.' The troll licked her lips, imagining how this traveller might taste, rolled in butter, seasoned with salt and sugar, and afraid. She believed that fear was the best flavour in all the wide world!

'That would be very kind of you.' Said the tin soldier, and followed the troll into her castle.

Well, beloved, the tin soldier wasted no time in darting off, and hiding in the depths of that great and ugly castle, where the bricks were black and wet, and the carpets made of sharp twigs and ice. Even flames did not burn hot in that place, so cursed was it, by troll magic.

He hid, and went exploring, and evaded the troll woman, who roared and wailed in anger at losing her meal! She thundered down passages, and up into towers, and across her wide halls in search of the lost traveller; the tin soldier. But he was too small and nimble for her - and so stayed out of sight.

Well, beloved, he had run out of his one and half thoughts. He needed more! Now that he was within the troll castle, and close enough to attempt to kill her - how on Earth could it be done? She was huge, and tough, and fearsome! His little brain ticked like an old clock, my beloved, yes indeed, as he slowly allowed another one and a half thoughts into his head.

'Hello to you, and what are you?' Asked a bug, crawling on a wall. It was black and shiny as a raisin, with wings that buzzed and big dark eyes.

'Hello to you. I am a tin soldier,' Said the tin soldier, 'And I am here to kill the evil troll, and free from her belly the wife of the man who made me, and set free all the lost travellers that are pricked, and bound, and stacked in the dungeons below.'

'A noble quest indeed!' Said the bug, 'I have a thousand brothers and sisters, also trapped within this castle. We hide in the dark corners and high rafters to avoid being squashed flat by the evil old troll. If you need aid of any kind, we shall provide it!'

The tin soldier shook the bug's many hands, and they hatched a plan!

Further on his secret travels through the troll castle, the little tin soldier met a spider woman, weaving.

'Hello to you, and what are you?' Asked the spider woman, her many red eyes blinking and winking in all directions.

'Hello to you. I am a tin soldier,' Said the tin soldier, 'And I am here to kill the evil troll, and free from her belly the wife of the man who made me, and set free the lost travellers that are pricked, and bound, and stacked in the dungeons below.'

'A very fine quest, indeed!' Said the spider woman, 'I have a thousand children, also fearful of the evil old troll woman - for she does love to pull off our many legs, and squash us flat! If you need aid of any kind, we shall provide it!'

The tin soldier shook the spider woman's many hands, and they hatched a plan!

And so, beloved, the tin soldier continued his exploration of the castle, up and up and up into a high tower.

'Hello to you, and what are you?' Came a shrill voice from high above. It was a bird; a dusty, moth-eaten old bird with a bright orange bill.

'Hello to you. I am a tin soldier,' Said the tin soldier, 'And I am here to kill the evil troll, and free from her belly the wife of the man who made me, and set free all the lost travellers that are pricked, and bound, and stacked in the dungeons below.'

'A mighty good quest, indeed!' Said the bird, 'I have a thousand cousins, and all of us live in fear of the troll woman, for she takes our eggs and plays at sports with them - smashing and squashing them all! If you need aid of any kind, we shall provide it!'

The tin soldier shook the bird's foot, for birds do not have hands, and they hatched a plan!

Onward, the tin soldier went, climbing up and sliding down, shuffling through cracked bricks, and eventually finding his way to the dungeon!

'Hello to you, and what are you?' Said a voice in the dark. It was a black cat. But oh dear not just any black cat - a huge savage thing that the troll woman kept as a slave, guarding the dungeon! But the little tin soldier hadn't thoughts enough to understand the danger before him.

'Hello to you. I am a tin soldier,' Said the tin soldier, 'And I am here to kill the evil troll, and free from her belly the wife of the man who made me, and set free all the lost travellers that are pricked, and bound, and stacked in the dungeons below.'

Now, beloved, cats are cunning things, and so it said to the tin soldier, 'Oh my, what a quest!' And he swished his tail one way, and the other, 'I have a thousand friends, also slaves to the evil troll, who live in fear of her boots and bad tempers. If you need aid of any kind, we shall provide it.'

The tin soldier shook the cat's paw, and they hatched a plan!

Well, beloved, the tin soldier waited quietly and secretly until nightfall. Through a high window a full moon shone, and snow began to fall, as the terrible troll woman slept. Her snores and grunts shook the very bones of the Earth, and this is when the attack was launched.

First the bugs - they flew in her ears and up her nose. She awoke with such a clatter and a splatter! She wailed and cursed, and crunched down on the bugs. But that wasn't the end of it. No! Next the spider woman and her thousand children crawled upon her, weaving their nets and ropes about her shaggy hide. Though the spider ropes were strong, they were no match for the troll and her magic. She conjured a light that burned away the bugs, and her fingers became knives that sliced and diced the spider ropes to pieces.

The birds took their turn next, the thousand feathered cousins beat at the old troll with their wings, hoping to push her from her high bedroom window - but she used her magic to make her feet heavy as millstones, and so could not be pushed out. She tore at the birds, plucking them in the air as they flew about.

The tin soldier, saddled upon the savage black cat, rode into the battle next. But he was betrayed!

The cats caught the birds and ate them up, and the savage black beast upon whose back the tin soldier rode, presented him to his mistress.

'This is a tin soldier,' Said the cat, 'And he is here to kill you dead, and free from your belly the wife of the man who made him, and set free all the lost travellers that are pricked, and bound, and stacked in the dungeons below.'

Well, beloved, can you imagine how the old troll woman shrieked? She snatched up the tin soldier in her claws, and screamed and bellowed in rage and triumph.

'You shall be my prisoner!' She said, 'And as punishment for your attempting to kill me, you shall be kept in a cage, and every night you must watch as I dine on the travellers that I have pricked, and bound, and stacked in my dungeon below!'

And that is exactly what she did, that cruel old troll.

Every day, she made him watch, as another traveller was brought up from the dungeon, rolled in butter, seasoned with salt and sugar, and gobbled up! The tin soldier was beside himself - he didn't know what to do!

By and by, beloved, as the weeks and months passed, the tin soldier learned that the evil troll had a daughter, who had fire for hair, and whose skin was as white as snow. He never saw her, for she was kept always elsewhere in the castle. But with every passing day, he grew more and more in love with her. How could that be, you ask, if he had never met her? Well, do not forget that he can only have one and a half thoughts at a time! He fell in love with what he imagined of her! Radiant beauty, a delicate singing voice, a gentle touch, and a kind heart. He was forgetting, of course, that she too was a troll.

One day, after the old troll woman had devoured another buttered, salted, sugared, terrified traveller, she sat licking her fingers when her daughter called on her. The tin soldier was amazed - for she was every bit as beautiful as he had imagined, and more besides! But the old troll woman flew into a rage.

'Dinner time is a private time!' The old troll roared, 'You were commanded never to look upon me eating, unless a terrible punishment befall you!'

Though trolls are vile and tricky creatures, with terrible and disgusting eating habits, they hate to be observed as such - for through their magic they are forced to see themselves as the beasts they wish they were not. And so when dining, the troll mother ate alone. Now, you may ask why she allowed the tin soldier to remain. Well, beloved, he had only spots of solder for eyes, and the troll magic did not recognise them as true eyes, though they served him as such very well indeed.

The troll daughter had spent years obeying her mother, until she eventually learned via the whispers of the bugs, and the spiders, and the birds, of the tin soldier and his quest. She had grown curious of the little man who was so daring as to kill her mother! Her curiosity had won over her wits, and, disobeying her mother, she had entered the old troll's dining hall.

The troll mother roared, slamming down her fork, and the weeping traveller upon its tines. She snatched up her daughter, and placed her within the cage with the tin soldier.

'Now you shall live in this cage,' The old troll said, 'Never to eat, and always to watch me eat! You shall live forever hungry and alone!' The old troll woman placed this curse on her daughter. And she had quite forgotten the tin soldier was even there, he had been so still and quiet all this time.

Days passed, then weeks, and the tin soldier tried to become a friend to the troll daughter.

'Hello to you. I am a tin soldier,' Said the tin soldier, 'And I am imprisoned here due to my plan to kill your troll mother, and free from her belly the wife of the man who made me, and set free all the lost travellers that are pricked, and bound, and stacked in the dungeons below.'

But the troll daughter ignored him. And ignored him. And ignored him.

She was a mysterious troll, that flame haired little girl. Beautiful, unlike her mother, small, unlike her mother, and quiet, unlike her mother. But, beloved, this hid the fact that she was a much more terrible and ferocious troll than her mother!

When, one day, her mother had eaten her fill of buttered, salted, and sugared travellers, the daughter called out 'Mother, I have watched you eat one hundred men and women, and now my own hunger is blazing like a furness.' The troll daughter cast a mighty spell, and the cage around them vanished. She, and the tin soldier fell to the floor, where he hid from the terrible trolls.

The two of them fought a great battle using unspeakable troll magics. The troll mother was old and weak, but cunning. And the troll daughter was young and strong, and wily. They fought for a day and a night, as around them their castle began to crumble.

Then, beloved, oh goodness me - the final magic battle took place! The mother troll swallowed her daughter whole, but within her stomach the daughter opened her own mouth and swallowed her mother from within! Then the mother did the same, and the daughter once more! On and on this went, until they had swallowed each other so many times that one could not be told from the other. They became a single ever-gulping shape with a dark shaggy pelt, ferocious brazier hair, and claws like sickles.

But, dear beloved, what of the tin soldier? He had not been idle all the while - no! As the two trolls devoured each other, the travellers fell from the stomachs into which they had been swallowed. Hundreds of them poured out, and they ran! The tin soldier guided them through the castle to safety, to the road beyond the castle, to freedom.

Can you imagine it, beloved? The quaking castle, falling to rubble all around? The buttered, salted, and sugared travellers running for their lives, having been gobbled up - suddenly free! And the tin soldier, with only one and a half thoughts in his head, trying to think what to do next?

The trolls fought like a whirlwind, like ice and fire, gulping each other down whole again and again and again - until eventually their bellies were empty of travellers, and out fell the old soldier's wife. Alive, but buttered and salted and sugared. The tin soldier rushed to her aid.

'Hello to you. I am a tin soldier,' Said the tin soldier, 'And I am here to kill the evil troll, and free you from her belly, for you are the wife of the man that made me, and set free all the lost travellers that are pricked, and bound, and stacked in the dungeons below.'

The wife was ever so grateful, though sad to learn of her husband's passing. Together they opened up the dungeon, and removed the pins, untied the ropes, and took down the travellers stacked five bodies deep on the shelves. The travellers ran, and ran, and escaped the crumbling castle.

From the road beyond the castle, the tin soldier and the old wife watched the trolls bury themselves. They made for themselves a tomb, using the bricks and mortar of their own castle, piled high and round and crooked as themselves. The bugs fled, the spiders fled, the birds fled, and the cats fled. The travellers were freed, and the trolls, finally, were dead.

'A mighty successful quest,' Said the tin soldier, 'Though it did not go as I had imagined it would.'

And the old woman, wife to the one who had made him, cradled the little tin soldier to her bosom and cried magical tears. They had been given powers from her having spent so long in the belly of the mother troll - and these magic tears made the tin soldier into her husband - no longer dead, beloved! - and they went home, and lived happily ever after...

Chapter Seven
Fragments

From his hiding place under Greta's bed, Pevril quietly sang, "Miss Molly was a dolly who was sick, sick, sick. So Greta called for the doctor to come quick, quick, quick. The doctor came with his bag and his hat. And he knocked on the door with a ..." He went suddenly mute as someone knocked on the Toy Hospital door, rat-a-tat-tat.

He heard the footfalls of Greta and Sylvia bustle down the stairs, and the squeak of the Toy Hospital door opening and closing. Emerging from his hiding place, he made his way slowly back towards the living room. There she was, high up on the coffee table; Little Miss Molly Radish.

As he stood there watching her, little miss Molly Radish turned to face him and said, "Boo."

Pevril ran away, and Molly giggled. There was something about the dolly that the remnant of Pevril Pudding did not like. There was too little left of the man for the tin soldier to contemplate too deeply what another possessed toy might mean for the Toy Hospital. Focussed almost entirely on retaining his freedom, he climbed into a crack in a wall, where mice and rats had made narrow secret tunnels about the building, and there he hid.

Greta and Sylvia returned to the living room, confused and irritable. Miss Moss and her odd photography project had spooked them slightly.

"We need to find where that little so-and-so has hidden himself." Sylvia declared, matter-of-fact, hands on her hips, surveying the room, and the empty bird cage, "We can't have official spook detectors coming and discovering him. They'll probably have to burn the Hospital down to purge his spirit."

"You've been watching too many scary films." Though dismissive of Sylvia's concern, Greta picked Molly Radish up from the coffee table and began to wind her red hair around her fingers, "It's bad enough having one ghost loitering..." Greta trailed off, clenching her dentures.

Sylvia eyed her friend curiously, the half finished sentence hanging in the air.

"You'll be miffed at me." Greta said, putting Molly back on the coffee table, "But I broke your mirror."

*

Greta explained everything as briefly as she could, while Sylvia's eyes grew wider and wider.

"You spoke to her!" Sylvia's jaw hung open.

"I didn't much care for her, truth be told." Greta sniffed.

In a flash, Sylvia was away to her room. She threw open the box, knocking the puzzle box onto the floor in her haste, where it rolled under her bed. Into the pink velvet went Sylvia's hands, and out came the cracked mirror. The only reflection was Sylvia's own.

Greta joined Sylvia, and sniffed, "So you're not miffed with me?"

Sylvia rolled her eyes, "In future just ask what I want for Christmas pressies. But no, you dafty, I'm not."

"Pressies?" Greta asked, "Plural? You'll be lucky if you get one, the way things are going.

We've got a damned haunted house on our hands!"

"This is a house of fragments." Said the reflection of Angelica Tiffin, "Not a haunted house." Her reflection stepped between the two old women, and paced the small room.

Greta put her hands on her hips, "Nice of you to show up."

Angelica curtseyed in a way that Greta found quite patronising.

"Oh my goodness!" Sylvia exclaimed, "It's really you! You look just like I remember you!"

"Naturally. I'm hardly going to leave behind a haggard old spectre of myself am I? That's simply not my style."

"How are you?" Sylvia asked.

"Dead. So about as bored as you would expect."

"Right. Yes. Can't imagine there's much in the way of social lives for ghosts and whatnot." Sylvia muttered.

"You'd be surprised!" Angelica smiled ruefully.

"Greta said you've a message for me?" Sylvia asked, "Is it that I'm a witch? I knew I was. I could feel it in my waters. All my life I've known I was different!"

"No." Angelica said, "My message is not that you're a witch. You'd have shown signs by now."

"Oh." Sylvia was deflated.

"Accidentally levitated some cutlery lately?"

"Not that I'm aware of."

"Given an animal the power of speech?"

"I don't think so. Where's Clive? He meaws in a certain way for kippers. Does that count?"

"Managed to raise an army of the dead, turn water into wine, or fly?"

"Oh goodness me, no!"

Angelica nodded, "Then I can categorically say that you, my dear Sylvia, are not a witch."

"Shame." Sylvia said.

"It's not all it's cracked up to be, honestly." A dark look passed over Angelica's face, brought on perhaps by some painful memory. Greta was about to open her mouth and ask the spectral flapper to elaborate, but Sylvia got in first.

"Right. So what's the message?" She asked.

Angelica looked at her cousin with a serious set to her drawn-on eyebrows, "Now, this message came to me from a good friend; Another witch, who had the power of foresight. It was important enough for her to write it down in one of her special books. I held onto it for years, and nothing came of it. However, as I was approaching my end..."

*

An old Angelica Tiffin opened her eyes. The milky white of increasing blindness, and her paper-thin skin made her seem to already be a ghost. She was much faded from the vivacious young woman in the mirror.

"Is there someone there?" She croaked, her voice almost a whisper.

A visitor sat on the bed beside her, someone who was not there. Someone with their hair pulled up into a bun on the top of her head, and an apron lashed like a sail about her middle.

"It's me." Said the ghost at Angelica's side.

"Nelly?" The old Angelica smiled, "Come to wish me well on my way out the door?"

The ghost called Nelly, the ghost of the witch who could foretell the future, leant forward and kissed her friend on the forehead, "I've unfinished business, it seems." She said, "The only one of my visions which hasn't happened yet."

Angelica nodded feebly, "I know the one."

"You need to make sure it's passed on, and that she's warned. If not, I fear the worst."

On matchstick arms, Angelica pushed herself up into a sitting position, "Pass me my hand mirror?" She indicated the item, laid on her vanity across the room. Nelly fetched it for her.

"Can you do me a favour?" Angelica asked, as she began to fuss with her much-thinned hair in the mirror.

"I can try." Nelly was always willing to go above and beyond for her friends, though never said so explicitly.

"Call Mr Patchouli in, in about ten minutes?"

Nelly nodded, and waited the ten minutes. In that time Angelica wrote a note, and then using the last spark of her magic, pulled from deep down inside, she broke off a piece of herself, a shimmering sliver of silver, and pushed it into the hand mirror. When that was done, she died, and the ghost at her bedside called for the undertaker.

"Mr Patchouli?" She called, "Could you come in here, please?" And then she vanished.

*

"So what's the message? What's the vision?" Greta asked impatiently.

"Sit down. It's in the form of a fable. It's called the Sorry Tale of the Tin Soldier and the Troll."

Greta refused to sit, but Sylvia plonked herself down onto her bed, rapt. The story unravelled line by line, paragraph by paragraph, until Greta too had to sit down. When Angelica finished, Sylvia felt the urge to applaud.

Greta gnashed her falsies, "But what does it mean?" She snapped, "It's clear that the troll in the story is me!"

"Is it?" Angelica raised an eyebrow, "That is interesting."

Greta was infuriated! She was confounded! She was vexed!

"This is daft." She said, wagging a finger at the mirror, "We can't be taking this seriously? A second-hand prophecy from a ghost!"

Angelica rolled her eyes, "Ghosts aren't real."

"They're not?" Sylvia was confused.

"Well, they are," Angelica continued, "But they're not spirits, or the soul of the departed, or demonic entities. Ghosts are the memory of a person. As insubstantial as a reflection, on the whole."

"Now hang on." Sylvia said, "What about Pevril? He's not just memories! He tried to kill Greta!"

"Who?" Angelica laughed, "Who's Pevril? And from what I've seen of your friend, she looks tough as old leather. Can't imagine her being easy to off."

"Well…" Sylvia began, but Greta interrupted.

"He's the ghost of my dead husband, and every year since he popped his smelly clogs he's been trying to kill me! He's trapped in a toy soldier."

Angelica took a deep breath in through her nose, and paused thoughtfully before she spoke again.

"Another piece of the prophecy puzzle! How can I simplify this so it makes sense to you?" Angelica tutted, pacing back and forth, "Buildings act like storage devices, they store up the memory of everything that happens inside their walls. The energy, the vibrations, the emotions, the happenings. They make a record of it all. The more emotionally charged the events that take place, the stronger the recordings are."

"Recordings? Like on a VHS player?" Sylvia queried.

"If I knew what a veeaychess was I might be able to answer that. Anyway, buildings are passive, just lumps of brick and mortar, soaking up everything, layered and muddled." She paused her pacing and held a finger aloft, "However! Toys are active. Toys are actively given memories, and emotion, and are incredibly powerful. Look up poppets, when you get a chance. You might find you have one or two in the Hospital without realising." She paused, and as both old women stared blankly at her for several seconds, she decided to fill the silence, "Ghosts don't often pop into being on their own. Something or someone powerful causes them to, oh what's the right word... manifest! Something causes a ghost to manifest."

Uncomfortable ideas began to creep into Greta's head, "If ghosts are just memories, and toys are vessels into which we pour our emotions... Are you saying that, somehow, I conjured the ghost of my dead husband to torture me? Why would I do that to myself?"

Angelica shrugged, "You would be the one to answer that particular conundrum. To return to my initial statement; there are no ghosts in your hospital. It't not a haunted house. But there are... fragments. Little tiny pieces that might conceivably be a thousand ghosts-in-waiting, if given the right encouragement. Each toy houses the memories of playtimes, of the love they experienced, and potentially the pain at being abandoned, or lost."

"How can you tell all this?" Sylvia asked breathily, incredulously.

"What do you suppose I am, hmm?"

"A fragment?" Greta guessed.

"And bingo was his name-oh!" Angelica clapped happily, overjoyed that they finally understood, "If you want to tame and defang the toy possessed by your dead husband, you have to find out why you brought him back in the first place." Her image began to fade from the mirror, "I'm tired. Manifesting takes up a lot of energy. Good luck." And she was gone.

"No! Wait! Come back!" Sylvia pleaded, tapping the glass of the mirror urgently, "You can't go yet!"

"Fat load of help she was." Greta sniffed.

Sylvia stared at her reflection in the hand mirror, a scowl creasing her brow. She was all shaken up inside.

"I really wanted to be a witch." She muttered.

She felt like her world was suddenly topsy-turvy and inside out. A fairytale prophecy had been given to her that sounded very much like, at least in part, the trials and tribulations of Greta and Pevril Pudding. But why had it been given to her? She looked up at Greta, and felt a strange fearful pang in her chest. What was that feeling?

Sylvia pushed it away, and clutched the mirror tightly.

"I think I need a cup of tea." She said.

19th of December.

For the best part of two days Sylvia had made herself busy, keeping out of Greta's way. The prophetic tale of Greta as a terrible troll had stuck with her, like something caught in the back of her throat. No matter how she swallowed or fidgeted her tongue, the strange feeling remained. It was invasive. It made her consider her oldest friend in a new light, and she began to feel, crumb by crumb, unsafe.

As she moved about the Hospital, dusting, and arranging, and adjusting price labels, and so on, she eyed the toys warily. Each one of them could house a ghost-in-waiting. What encouragement might they take to spring to life? She looked into button eyes, and watched for any sign of movement. She prodded stuffed tummies to see if it'd cause a giggle.

"What are you doing?" Greta had been watching her friend bustle strangely about, from her perch on the stool behind the counter.

"Nothing." Sylvia said, straightening up and trying to act natural, which made Greta all the more suspicious.

"You looking for the escaped convict?"

"Hmm?"

"Pevril."

"Oh!" Sylvia had almost forgotten about him, "Yes, yes I was."

Greta nodded, "I've searched the place from top to bottom and back up again. He's nowhere to be found."

"He is quite small," Sylvia said, "I suppose he could fit into all kinds of nooks and crannies."

"Every night I hear him down here, knocking things over, bumping about. Every morning something else is overturned, or a display is all a mess. This morning the cupboard door was open again."

Sylvia looked at the cupboard, "I wonder why he's causing such a ruckus at night."

"To keep me awake and wondering, no doubt." Greta said, "To stop me from sleeping! Where's that cat?"

The change of topic momentarily confused Sylvia, and she shrugged, "Somewhere. Maybe having a nap on my bed. Why?"

"You'd think he'd be more use, chasing and catching the little pest." Greta held up a wind-up mouse, freshly fixed and decorated with a little ribbon around its neck, "One more on my to-do list, and that's me finished for the year."

Sylvia was conflicted. She was wary of her friend, but couldn't understand why. Here was a woman who celebrated the wondrous playthings of children, who fixed them, and loved them with as much passion as if they were her own. Yet the prophecy niggled. It scratched relentlessly at the back of her brain.

*

In Sylvia's room, Clive the cat lay on his back across her bed, snoring contentedly. He shifted in his sleep, stretching out his legs, curling his tail.

Ding.

Clive woke up, and his ears flicked back and forth, triangulating the source of the sound. He sat up and, using a licked paw, began to groom his face.

Ding.

Like oscillating radar dishes, his ears narrowed down the origin of the sound. Below. He slithered from the bed and peered underneath, his one good eye opening wide in the dim light.

The puzzle box.

It had expanded, the outer corners having pulled apart, revealing the various clockwork segments within. The top remained one solid sheet, and the crank handle slowly turned. It turned under the stubby porcelain fingers of Little Miss Molly Radish. With her other hand she held up a finger to her painted lips and whispered, "Sshh."

The cat hissed, and arched his back. Taking a couple of steps away, he kept his eye glued to the dolly, as she slowly wound. As the handle performed a full circle, something inside the puzzle box went ding.

*

Furious Crumpet came to call on Sylvia Garland. She had dolled herself up and slapped on a little too much make-up, in Greta's opinion, and arm in arm they sauntered away up the street. Greta watched them go from the open doorway of the Hospital. The snow banks and ice sheets seemed not to bother them, as they drifted into the evening darkness.

Alone in the Hospital, with jolly Christmas lights twinkling everywhere, and the happy faces of puppets and teddies and dolls all about her, Greta felt a strange darkness. She didn't like being alone. Her own company she enjoyed very much, but being alone? Not one jot. She locked the door, and flipped the sign to 'Closed'. Clive the cat sat watching her from the counter, his eye narrowed.

"I still don't like cats." She said, as she tickled him gently behind the ears, "How about we share a couple of my fancy kippers?"

Clive meowed happily.

*

The restaurant was half full, and waiters ambled about trying to look busy, waiting for glasses to refill and plates to clear.

"I'm just not sure what I think about it all." Sylvia said.

Crumpet lifted his hand from hers as she stopped talking, and began stroking his chin, "How very... interesting." He said.

Sylvia wasn't sure what had come over her, but she had had the sudden urge to tell Crumpet everything. Everything! She had rattled it all off, while he sat there, holding her hand; Pevril, the flies and spiders and birds and cats, the casket, the mirror, the dolly from the cupboard, Angelica Tiffin, and the fairy tale prophecy. Through it all he simply nodded, and was attentive. He didn't laugh at her, or scoff, or tut at her; the silly old woman and her story.

"Sorry," She said, "I don't think I was supposed to tell you all that. Greta will be angry I've told you."

"I can keep a secret." He said, lifting his glass of wine and taking a sip.

"You believe me?" Sylvia asked cautiously.

Crumpet shrugged, "I've seen much of this world, so I know that nothing is impossible."

"So you don't believe me? You're humouring me?"   Sylvia sagged in her seat, fidgeting with her wine glass.

"If you truly do not feel entirely safe there, why not move out?" He took another sip, watching her intently over the cut-glass rim.

"I couldn't possibly! I promised. It's me and Greta until the end, in that place. If I left, I don't think Greta could cope. She's not actually as strong as she makes out. She might seem a tough old nut, but that shell is paper thin."

Crumpet nodded, "Could have fooled me."

"It's a bit of an act, really. She's a pussy cat."

"If it's an act, who is she performing for?"

Sylvia sighed, "Herself, I suppose. She's never had it very easy, all things considered. So she acts tough and resilient to convince herself that she is. Bet that sounds a load of codswallop to you. But I've known her since we were teenagers." She paused to take a gulp of her wine, "Still... I'm rattled. After everything that's happened recently…" She trailed off, sighing.

"What would make you feel safer, more contented?" Crumpet put down his glass as their starters arrived. Soup of the day with crusty bread and little squares of butter.

"Honestly, I'm not sure." Sylvia tore her bread into little chunks, dropping them into her soup to soak.

Crumpet spooned a thin layer of the brownish concoction between his lips, and nodded appreciatively, "There is one solution that comes to mind."

Sylvia began poking at the soaking bread with her spoon, "Oh yes?"

"A temporary measure, only." He said, raising a finger.

"Mm-hmm?"

"Until all this, whatever it is, is over and done with."

"Right?"

"And you're welcome to say no to the idea."

Sylvia stared at Crumpet, confused and wary of what he might suggest. He really was terribly handsome, sat there with his hair slicked back and his magenta suit. Always impeccably dressed, and those eyes of his! They flashed charm and danger in equal measure, making her a little hot under the collar. She felt a mediterranean sunset on the horizon; a soft peach sky wheeling with gulls and sailboat masts.

"Spit it out." She said.

He put down his spoon and rested his hand on hers, "Perhaps I could move in with you, for just a little while. *Sì?*"

"Yes." The word was out of her mouth before she even thought about it.

"Magnificent." He said, taking back his hand and spooning more soup under his pristine moustache, "I will come around tomorrow with some things."

Sylvia's heart fluttered with girlish excitement, and she gulped down the last of her wine. It didn't occur to her until the walk home after the fourth course, quite what Greta might have to say on the matter of sharing their home with her fancy man. But by that point she had finished most of a bottle of mediocre chardonnay, and wasn't overly concerned.

"Piffle to what Greta says about it." She slurred happily, giggling, as she unlocked the Hospital door and fell over the door mat.

Crumpet helped her up, ever the gentleman, and kissed her goodnight.

Sylvia would have skipped up the stairs, she felt so light and giddy, but her wine-addled feet could only manage a shuffle. She made her way to her room, where in the yellow light of her reading lamp, reality set in. She sat down heavily on her bed, and worried if she had made the right decision. Tiredness overcame her, and before long she was laid in bed, snoring and muttering.

*

20th of December.

Sylvia woke to her bedroom door slamming open, and the thunderous grind of Greta's voice, "You've got some explaining to do, Sylvia Garland!"

Woozily, Sylvia blinked, sat up, and tried to speak. Her throat was dry and no words came out.

"There's someone downstairs to see you, with two large suitcases and a toothbrush."

"What?" Sylvia's memories of the night before started to surface into her mind, and she went pale, "Oh dear." She said.

"Flagrant Trumpet is moving in? Is he? Is that so?" Greta was almost screaming, visibly shaking with rage.

"I'll deal with it." Sylvia said, "With him. I'll deal with him." Throwing off the covers, she shuffled into her slippers and hurried downstairs.

Greta seethed, her frail fists clenched tightly. Taking a few deep breaths, she unclenched, and made her way to the living room, where she began to pace back and forth. She strained her ears to listen to the conversation downstairs, but could only hear muttered words. Each time she reached the window, she pressed her face against it and peered down, hoping to see Crumpet turned out onto the street, dismissed. But with each lap of the room, she became more and more concerned.

Sylvia was not turning him away. Was that man truly here to stay?

"How could she do this without talking to me?" She ground her dentures, as she peered out into the street again.

"It was very spur of the moment." Crumpet said behind her.

Greta spun around and pointed an accusing finger at him, "Was this your idea? I know your sort. Good for nothing, with magpie habits!"

Sylvia came into the room next, hands outstretched placatingly, "It's only for a little while, Greta. Just temporary."

"Why?" Greta spat, "Eh? Why does he need to move in?"

"It's a work thing." Crumpet said, "The lease on my accommodation has expired, but my work in the city continues. Unfortunately I am without lodgings until the new year."

Greta eyeballed him, "And what exactly is your work, Flatulent Crumble?"

"I work for the embassy."

"Which embassy?"

"Look," Crumpet sighed, "I will be out much of the day. You will hardly even notice that I'm here." He reached to take one of her hands, "You won't mind me being here, honestly. *Fidati di me.*"

Greta pulled her hand away before he finished speaking, and for a moment he looked very annoyed.

He recovered in the blink of an eye, and straightened himself, "Greta Pudding, you do not like me, which I cannot help. But that is your problem, not ours." He turned on his heel and left the living room.

Sylvia made an apologetic face and followed him from the room, saying, "Let me help you unpack. I'm sure if I shunt up my frocks there's room for your suits in the wardrobe."

Rat-a-tat-tat.

Someone rapped on the Toy Hospital door. Greta sighed loudly, "Now what!?"

*

Miss Moss gave a thin-lipped smile as Greta let her in. It was brief, and it wasn't friendly. Greta eyed up the odd girl, who once more was not dressed nearly enough to protect her from the cold outside.

"You should be careful. Walking about like that in this weather, you'll catch your death."

Miss Moss stalked through the Hospital, and deposited her large handbag on the counter with a thump, "Ms Pudding, do you deal with occult practitioners, otherworldly tradesmen, or generally suspicious individuals?"

Greta paused for a moment before replying, "I don't think I know what you mean."

She was still raging, and it was clouding her ability to think. She took a moment to gather herself, placing her rump carefully on the stool behind the counter, where she could address Miss Moss eye to eye.

"Have you been awoken by anything you would describe as having gone bump in the night?"

Greta shrugged.

"Just answer the question." Miss Moss tutted.

"I'll ask you to kindly speak to me in a less confrontational tone of phrase." Greta tried her best to control her temper, and to dismiss the frosty young girl with as much decorum as she could muster, which wasn't much, "I will not have you waltzing in here before I'm even out of my curlers, making accusations against my character!"

Miss Moss simply stared at the old woman, letting her rattle on.

"I demand to speak to your superior. That old fella you came in with? What was his name? Shiver?"

"Mister Silver is currently abroad."

"How nice for him."

"But I have as much authority as him, when it comes to these particular matters."

Greta knotted her fingers together, "And what exactly are the particulars of the matter? Hmm?"

Miss Moss changed tack. She turned away from Greta, and began stalking around the hospital, fingering toys intermittently, "I have learned, through trial and error, that a distorted lens will show what shouldn't be there." Miss Moss said.

"What shouldn't be where?" Greta asked.

"That's why I came by taking those photographs. What appear to be distortions, overexposures, double exposures, issues with focus, et cetera, when pieced together like a puzzle..."

"Yes?"

"They can reveal a hidden image. Something that cannot be seen with the naked eye. Something that isn't entirely there. Something that shouldn't be there."

The two of them locked eyes, and Greta wondered who this odd girl really was, who knew about ghosts and the haunted Toy Hospital. And she wondered about her employers at the Funeral Home For The Unusually Deceased, and what they might know, or suspect. Her thoughts were punctured by Miss Moss advancing on her suddenly, and grabbing at her handbag. From within she retrieved a shiny envelope. The kind you get from the Kodak shop with your holiday snaps in.

Miss Moss opened the envelope and spread the photographs out across the counter. Most of them were a distorted mess. As she had described, they were overexposed, underexposed, double exposed, and in places blank, "What do you make of all this?" She asked, not looking up.

"Not a great deal." Greta said, casting only a casual glance at the images.

"Watch." Miss Moss began to arrange the photographs, overlapping them, one over another. Piece by piece, like a hallucinogenic jigsaw, Greta saw the interior of the Hospital appear in those odd pictures, laid out flat like a pop-up-book yet to spring to life. But the Hospital in the images was distorted, and the colours were wrong, and there were dark gaps running all over the place. Greta scowled, unsure what she was supposed to be seeing. And then she realised. She put a hand to her mouth and tried not to clench her jaw. There were many dark areas, long and curling like tendrils around shelves, and over toys, and each and every one seemed to lead to the creaky cupboard door. Greta looked up at her beloved Hospital, then back to the flattened photographic version.

"What are those?" Greta asked quietly, tapping the nearest of the dark tendrils with a thin nail.

"I was hoping you could tell me." Miss Moss folded her arms and glared at her, "I will ask you once more; Do you deal with occult practitioners, otherworldly tradesmen, or generally suspicious individuals?"

"No. No. Often; But that's just the general public for you." Greta said, trying to buy thinking time.

Miss Moss pointed over her shoulder at the cupboard door, "And what do you keep in there?"

"Paint. Nails. Thread. Stuffing. Solder. Brushes. Tweezers. Tools of the trade." Greta said honestly.

"Do you mind if I take a look?"

"Yes. But you're going to anyway, aren't you?"

Miss Moss smiled that thin smile of hers again, and turned to face the cupboard. She strode over, and paused with her hand on the knob. She appeared to take a deep breath, preparing herself. For what? What did she expect to find?

Miss Moss yanked open the door, her whole body tense. But the inside of the cupboard was stacked up with everything Greta had described.

The hinges didn't even emit their usual eerie squeak.

"I oiled them yesterday." Greta said, "The hinges. Couldn't abide the noise they'd started making of late."

Miss Moss stepped into the cupboard and began rifling through the contents. Shelf by shelf she made a methodical check of every item. Eventually she came to the floor, and noticed the hole and the splintered skirting.

"What happened here?" She asked.

"Mice." Greta said.

There was still a collection of traps on the floor, so Miss Moss nodded. It was a plausible explanation.

"Nothing came out of that hole did it?" Miss Moss dusted herself down and closed the cupboard door.

"Why do you ask that?"

"You need to start trusting me. There's something occurring here that you can't explain, that maybe I can help with."

The plea for trust made Greta trust Miss Moss even less, "Is that so?"

"Did something come out of that hole?"

"What would it matter if something did?"

"It would matter a great deal, because if something came out of that hole," And here she looked pointedly at the photographs, and the lines of shadow that ran towards the cupboard door, "You're in a great deal of trouble."

Greta sniffed, "I think I can handle myself."

Miss Moss scowled. Did Greta detect a hint of worry on the young woman's face? A crack in her polished veneer?

"Be careful." Miss Moss said, "And don't trust anything you see, or hear. Things might not be quite as they seem." She gathered up her handbag and turned to leave.

"You're forgetting your pictures." Greta said.

"No I'm not. I'm leaving them with you." She pointed at the counter-top from the doorway, "Something's coming, or is already here, and unless you open up to me your life may be in danger."

The door bounced shut behind her.

The Toy Hospital

Rylan John Cavell

Chapter Eight
The Floral Arrangement

Christmas dinner for the last few years had been wonderful. Sylvia would cook up a little roast, while Greta read from a book of festive tales and sipped sherry. She made the most wonderful pigs in blankets. Apparently her secret was to hide a smidge of black pudding under the bacon.

They'd then settle in the living room with trays on their laps and eat while watching whatever entertainment had been prepared by the BBC that year. There would be the familiar faces of Terry Wogan and Noel Edmonds, maybe the Two Ronnies, and no doubt a Carry On film tucked somewhere in the schedule. Sylvia would laugh at all the rude jokes, and Greta would tut, but she still enjoyed them.

Then it would be time to set fire to the dessert, and drink Baileys until they snoozed the evening away, well fed, warmed by the electric fire and pleasant companionship; their gentle snores like the purring of a cat.

But this year Greta foresaw a damaged Christmas, a ruined Christmas, a stained and wrecked Christmas. She saw this as the shadow of Furious Crumpet's presence cast itself over the Toy Hospital.

"I'm not getting him anything for Christmas." Greta said, remembering that she had also neglected to get Sylvia anything.

"You don't have to." Sylvia sighed, smiling apologetically. She was very glad that her friend had calmed down, though why she kept flicking through a pile of weird photographs was unclear, "And it's only for a little while. Before you even know it he'll be gone again, and you'll even miss him! Guaranteed!"

"Don't hold your breath for that." Greta muttered.

"Like he says, he'll be out most of the day anyhow. You'll barely notice he's here."

"Bit quick."

"What?"

"Getting him moved in."

"Well, yes. Admittedly I did agree to it after a couple of glasses of wine, but I didn't actually expect him to turn up first thing in the morning with his cases!"

"He irks me." Greta folded her arms, "But what's done is done. He's here now, so I suppose I'd best deal with that. I'm not a happy lady, mind."

"I know, and I'm very sorry. I wish I could have had some time to talk to you about it. But, well, that didn't happen."

"No. It certainly didn't. And you know what my answer would have been? To send him off to a hotel! I'm sure his employers at the embassy could reach behind their sofa cushions for enough loose change for a room at a hotel, hmm?"

"I suppose. I hadn't thought of that."

"No. Oh well."

"But isn't it nice having a fuller house for the festive season?" Sylvia beamed, "I think it's lovely."

Greta shook her head, too tired to fight on any longer. She held her hands up in defeat.

Sylvia hugged her tightly, and swayed gently left and right, "I love you, Greta Pudding."

"You too." Greta mumbled through her friend's bosom. She was never one at home with the L word. It never felt like it quite fit right.

A short while later, Greta was done up in her coat and rain bonnet, her bag over her arm and her stick at the ready.

"I'm off for a little window shopping." She called up the stairs to Sylvia, "Shouldn't be too long."

Without waiting for a reply, she left the Hospital. Taking it slowly over the snow - which seemed fresh and crisp every morning, without ever a flurry having fallen - Greta made her way to a cafe across the road. She hurried as fast as she could to get inside, and plonked herself down at an empty table. She ordered a fizzy drink as a treat, and waited. She kept her coat and bonnet on, sipping her drink, with her attention laser-focussed on the Toy Hospital door. She was not off for a spot of window shopping. She had told a fib. She was engaging in a little espionage.

"I'd do well as a spy." Greta muttered to herself, and she burped a little from the bubbles in her drink, "Pardon me."

As she sat there waiting, her mind drifted over her conversation with Miss Moss earlier that morning. Molly the dolly had come out of that hole, but she was just a dolly. There was nothing out of the ordinary about her. Greta dismissed Miss Moss' words. The girl was clearly exaggerating.

Greta downed the rest of her drink in a hurry. There he was!

Furious Crumpet left the Toy Hospital, sauntering away up the street. Greta waited a minute or two, watching him go, then set off in pursuit. She wanted some answers from Mr Crumpet. Who was he? What did he do for work? Why was he keen on Sylvia? She felt bad to think it, but she still didn't believe that he found her attractive. Not that she wasn't, back in the day. But those days had long since faded to twilight. She'd never admit it, but Greta had been a little jealous of Sylvia's good looks, once upon a time.

She was sure that there was something behind Crumpet's wooing of her, some scheme that Greta felt honour-bound to uncover, to protect her friend, and protect herself, and protect the Hospital.

Being so close to Christmas, the streets were marked by clusters of intrepid shoppers, wrapped up against the cold in gloves and scarves and bobble hats. She navigated around them as best she could, and swiped at the ankles of those who she wanted to move from her path with her stick.

"Old lady coming through, have some respect. Honestly, the youth of today!" She tutted.

Always she kept Furious Crumpet in sight. If he turned a corner, she would turn the corner. If he paused to peer into a shop window, she paused, and waited for him to continue. He walked a criss-cross path through the city centre, and Greta began to wonder exactly where he was heading. They didn't seem to be on a direct path. It was a meandering, s-bend and curling path, which began to make Greta worried. Maybe he knew she was following him?

No. Impossible.

She had been very careful to not be noticed. Very careful indeed.

His circuitous path led them to St Ann's Square, and to the small church at the back of it that gave the square its name. Greta wondered if he'd be stopping by Ronnies for a drink or something to eat, but he passed by and headed towards the church.

He paused at the doors to St Ann's, and looked over his shoulder, "Would you like to come inside?"

Greta froze, "I'm not following you."

Crumpet laughed, "Yes you are."

"Fine, yes I am."

"You'd make a dreadful spy, you know. I could see you loitering behind me in the reflection of every shop window I passed." Greta filed that away to better skulk unnoticed in future. "So what do you want?"

Greta advanced on him, "I want answers to some questions. I was hoping you'd lead me to your place of work, but I see you've just led me in circles."

"Yes, I have. If I walked at my usual pace you'd not have been able to keep up. I walked slowly, especially for you." He smiled, "So you want answers? To which questions?"

"The following," Greta began, "What are you up to in my Hospital? What racket is it that you're running, getting my Sylvia all smitten?"

Crumpet laughed a little at her, which incensed the old woman.
She stepped forward and waved her stick at him, "You can take that smug look off your face. I know your sort. You mean us no good. I can see it in your eyes."

Crumpet held up a hand for forgiveness, "I apologise, Ms Pudding. But I suddenly realised something about you."

"Oh yes? And what's that?"

"You're a witch!" He clapped his hands together merrily, "It explains so much!"

"What?" Greta's mouth hung open, "What are you talking about?"

"That's why the Glamour doesn't properly work on you, and why you've been able to dodge my Charms." He shook his head amusedly, then his eyes went wide, "Oh but it's better than that, isn't it?"

She stared at him agog.

"You didn't even know!" He laughed heartily, clapping his hands together again.

Greta searched for words, and came up empty. She was a witch? Impossible! She'd have noticed something by now, wouldn't she?

"Now that I understand what you are, I will be able to better suit the Charms I use to my needs."

"And what are your needs?" Greta said.

"Well, they're not really my needs per se; But the needs of the one who I find myself in service to. Oh Greta Pudding, Christmas will never be the same again. Well, nothing will ever be the same again."

"What are you talking about?" Greta demanded, "What's going on, and how does it involve Sylvia?"

"She's inconsequential. Simply a means to access your Hospital, and what lays beyond it."

Greta scowled, struggling to keep up, anger rising in her chest, "Inconsequential? There is nothing inconsequential about Sylvia Garland!

She's good and kind, and you're taking advantage of her! I shan't have it."

"I'm sorry, Ms Pudding, but the Fates have a game in play. It is down to us players to shuffle about the board and perform our roles."

"Speak plainly, or I'll introduce the end of my stick to the side of your head!" She advanced a pace, attempting to look menacing.

Crumpet simply shrugged, "I'm talking about the end of the world. Well, the end of this world anyway. Mine will be fine."

"What?" Greta was dumbfounded.

"And I'm sorry, but I can't let you remember any of this." Crumpet darted forward, placed the tip of his index finger on her forehead and said, "*La memoria!*"

Her vision danced, broken momentarily into radiating kaleidoscope patterns. Greta stumbled, unsteady on her feet, dizzy, seasick. She rested on her walking stick and took a slow, deep breath as the dizziness passed. Blinking, she looked around. The sick feeling in her stomach subsided, and she puzzled as to what had made her feel so suddenly peaky.

"Bugger." She said, "Where's that scoundrel got to?" She looked around and could not see Crumpet anywhere. But Crumpet hadn't moved. He curled in his finger, and lowered his arm, smiling with one side of his mouth.

Turning about, Greta scanned the square for him, "He's gone! He was right there, I was right behind him!" Frustrated with herself, she banged her stick on the ground.

Crumpet winced as her stick slammed into his foot, "Damn you, crone!" He hissed through gritted teeth.

Muttering and grumbling, Greta turned on the spot and began to retrace her steps. Crumpet watched her go, before examining the dent in the top of his shoe.

From a distance, across the square, in a shop window, his reflection looked very much like he had horns.

Greta wandered across the city centre, muttering distractedly to herself. She was upset that she'd let Crumpet get away after trailing him so well! Maybe she wouldn't make such a good spy after all, she thought grumpily. She should stick to mending toys, and avoid espionage.

She hadn't been paying attention to where she was going, and found herself in Shude Hill, staring at the dirty window of a second-hand book shop. She needed to get a Christmas present for Sylvia, and she believed a book was always a brilliant gift idea, so she went inside. The door jangled noisily as it opened, as the back was hung with bells. At a small cash-desk, tucked at the back of the cramped shop, a man with two false hands looked up and nodded a hello, before returning to the book he had open on his lap. The book shop smelled of dust and mothballs, which made Greta sneeze. The man at the desk didn't react, and so Greta shuffled into the tightly packed shelves, blowing her nose on the handkerchief she kept up her sleeve.

She scanned the various section titles; art, biographies, culture, design, ecclesiastical studies, food, and so on. Eventually she found a small section labelled 'occult', and had a moment of déjà vu as she scanned the spines. The titles Charms and Potions for the Modern Housewife, Exorcising

Demons and other Ephemera, and The Cleansing of a Tainted Abode all drew her eye.

Sylvia muttered, 'hmm'ed and tapped her chin, as she examined the books, settling eventually on a slim volume titled in inlaid gold leaf, though almost faded beyond reading; The Practical Guide To Modern Witchcraft and Sorcery, compiled and edited by Eunice Koldings. Greta hoped Sylvia would like it.

The man at the cash-desk took her money and handed back the change with incredible dexterity, despite his two stiff plastic-moulded hands. Greta was particularly impressed with the way he wrapped the book neatly in brown paper and string.

Even if Sylvia wasn't a witch, as Angelica Tiffin said, Greta was sure she would appreciate the book. As she left the bookshop, the bells jangling abrasively in her ears, she wondered if she would ever get used to knowing that ghosts and witches existed. Life felt like a daydream, sweeping her along through a series of bizarre situations. A headache had crept upon her, and it sat over her eyes. She rubbed her forehead and set off for home.

*

Sylvia was busy at the till making a sale of a tiny mechanical merry-go-round, and some doll's house furniture to a female couple when Greta returned to the Hospital.

"There you are!" Sylvia beamed, "I thought I might have to send out a search party after you. You've been gone hours."

"Have I?" Greta scowled. She hadn't been gone all that long, had she? Turning and looking over her shoulder, she noticed the sun dipping low behind the rooftops of the city. It was mid-afternoon already. She had been gone much longer than she realised.

Sylvia noticed her friend's strange mood, "You ok, lovey?" She asked, as she handed the couple their change, and waved them off with a cheery 'toodle-oo'.

"I've a riot of a headache."

"Oh no."

"Think I'll take myself up for an early night. Try and sleep it off."

"You want me to bring you up some cocoa?"

Greta nodded distractedly as she shuffled past, "That'd be very nice, thank you."

Sylvia watched her friend climb the steep stairs, still in her coat and rain bonnet, leaning on her stick, and seeming to struggle more than usual. Concern creased Sylvia's brow, and she chewed a fingernail, hoping that moving Crumpet in hadn't affected her friend more than she was letting on. She busied herself with the kettle, making Greta a big mug of cocoa. She melted a square of Dairy Milk into it for good measure. She was sure chocolate was medicinal. She'd read it in a magazine one time.

*

Sylvia left the steaming drink on Greta's bedside table. She was already drifting off to sleep. Creeping out, she closed the door and whispered, "Have happy dreams."

Turning around, she got a fright. The dark shape of a man stood in the corridor before her. It was Furious Crumpet.

"Sorry," He said, "Did I make you jump?"

Sylvia fanned with a hand, "I didn't hear you coming up the stairs. Gave me a fright!" She chuckled at her skittishness.

"My apologies." He gave a small bow, "I was wondering, my darling, where the puzzle box is that I gave you?"

Sylvia thought for a moment, "It's in my bedroom. Somewhere."

*

"Here it is!" Sylvia said, straightening up from her bedroom floor, "Oh, it's changed shape."

She held up the puzzle box and he examined it, "Have you been trying to solve the puzzle?" He asked, taking it from her.

"No, actually." Sylvia admitted, her cheeks flushing with embarrassment, "But it was just a cube when you gave it to me. Now look at it."

He turned it this way and that, examining its expanded size, the exposed clockwork mechanisms within, and the crank handle that protruded from one side. He smiled at her, "I'm glad you hadn't lost it."

"Must've been the cat. He likes knocking stuff off shelves. Came back to find him kicking all my perfume bottles across the room the other day. He's an adorable little mischief."

"That's cats, I suppose." Crumpet toyed with the crank handle of the puzzle box.

"Is it a jack-in-the-box?" Sylvia asked, "As that's what it looks like. A sophisticated mechanical jack-in-the-box."

"You'll have to wait and see." Crumpet left her bedroom, taking the puzzle box with him. He went to the living room and placed it on the coffee table next to Miss Molly Radish, "Now, don't go misplacing it again." He said gently, as Sylvia followed him in. He tapped her playfully on the nose.

She smiled, and as his eyes locked with hers, she felt that wonderful feeling that being near him seemed to create; the taste of tapas and red wine, a passionate Tango under star-lit skies, the flair of a Bull-fighter's cape. She giggled girlishly, and looked away, bashful for a moment. Then she took hold of his lapels and kissed him passionately, pressing herself against him. He seemed surprised by her lunge toward him for a moment, but yielded to her touch. When eventually she came up for air she said, "Bedroom. Now." And dragged him off.

Thankfully the noises that followed did not wake Greta from her deep sleep.

*

The rhythmic snoring of two old women filled the Toy Hospital, as the moon shone bright in the late December sky. Crumpet made his way in bare feet to the living room, and pulled open the curtains, letting in the moonlight. His pyjamas were black embroidered silk, and they glistened like oil.

He sat in the chair by the window, and crossed one leg over the other, staring at the puzzle box and the dolly beside it, bathed in pearly midnight moon-glow.

"How would you prefer I addressed you?" He enquired of the dolly, "Your Maleficence? Your Unholy Majesty? Your Creepiness?"

Little Miss Molly Radish seemed to smile, though her porcelain face did not shift, "You may call me... Everything." She said in a high pitched girlish voice, and she giggled.

Crumpet dipped his head in a brief nod of respect, "I am at your service, oh Everything."

Molly stood stiffly onto her little painted shoes, "I am aware of this. It was you who fetched me a key."

Crumpet reached forward and tapped the puzzle box, "Another day or so and it will have tuned in precisely to your pocket reality."

"I grow impatient."

"With all due respect, you've waited how long already? Why the rush now?"

"I have waited..." Molly shook her head, "Too long. Like a dawn that craves to break, I have dwelt in the Abject Void, waiting, longing, hungry for release! The proximity of escape excites me."

The child's voice uttering words the like of which Crumpet had only heard from certain occult elders gave him a strange thrill.

"But it was not I that summoned you." Said Molly, looking at Crumpet with unblinking glass eyes, "To whom do you pledge servitude?"

"To you."

Molly scoffed, "I know your breed, horned one! You sprang from deceit and dirt, fire and bitterness. You are fickle as the wind. To whom do you pledge servitude?"

"My employer pledges allegiance to you, and therefore so do I. In a roundabout way."

Molly tilted her head slightly, curiously, "And this employer understands the consequences of my release?"

"Yes indeed." Crumpet lied. He had in fact been told very little. He hid that effortlessly.

"How interesting." Molly giggled, "And delightful!" She rubbed her porcelain hands together greedily.

From a hole in the skirting board, Pevril Pudding, unobserved, took in everything that was being said, though understood very little.

"My ability to remain in this form begins to diminish." Molly said, "That is why I am impatient. If I am not freed soon, I must wait another untold number of millennia until the conjunction of this world, and the Abject Void."

Crumpet nodded, smiling a half smile, "I suspected something of the sort. What do you need in order to maintain your presence?"

"I need to consume phantasmal energies. I devoured the crumbs within the massed items in the chamber below."

"The toys?"

"They were insufficient. I attempted to devour the fragment within the tin soldier while we were incarcerated, but he fought back and escaped."

"That must have been quite irritating."

Molly stared at Crumpet, who shook his head, amused.

"Perhaps this will suffice?" From his pyjama pocket he pulled a hand mirror.

In the cracked glass of the hand mirror, Angelica Tiffin peered at him and scowled, "You!" She exclaimed, "What are you doing with my mirror?"

"She knows you." Molly said.

Crumpet nodded, "We were acquainted, while she was alive."

"You're a bounder and a cad!" Angelica was furious, "Sylvia! Greta!" She shouted.

Crumpet presented the mirror to Molly Radish and said, "*Buen provecho.*"

Molly Radish reached out with stubby porcelain hands towards the mirror.

"Get away!" Angelica cried out, panic in her voice, "Sylvia! Help!"

Molly Radish reached into the broken glass of the mirror.

"No!" Angelica vanished.

Molly Radish pulled a sliver of silver from the mirror; a flickering, dancing fragment of light. Then she opened her mouth and ate it.

*

Greta tossed and turned in her sleep. She dreamed a tangled jumble of dreams. Moments of fantasy wove themselves into her memories, that dissolved into others, that collapsed into others.

Through these dreams, her memories seemed to unspool, released from the tight coil in which she had wound them, bound them up, locked them away. Each of them unpleasant, and as fresh now as if they had just been lived; The death of her parents while still young. The maiden aunt who raised her with little care. The man who abused her one day, and the back-street surgeon who rid her of the results of that encounter. Meeting Pevril, their romance, the war. His return, their marriage, and their slow descent into resentment. Her refusal to act on his nocturnal impulses, caused by the painful memories of the surgeon and his viscous implements. The Toy Hospital. Pushing Pevril down the stairs. His nursery rhyme fixation. His sickness, and his death.

She woke up in a cold sweat, panting. Had she cried out? It felt like she had. But no one came running. Perhaps she hadn't, after all. Clive the cat looked up from the blanket at the foot of the bed, blinking slowly in the dark.

Greta wiped her face on the sleeve of her nightie, and hoped the dream would fade. But it didn't, it lingered. Her memories were free, released from their restraints, tangled and messy now, laying all higgledy-piggledy inside her head. Where once there had been order, now she was chaos. She was all of a dither, and couldn't decide whether or not to get up and shake off her odd feelings, or attempt to return to sleep.

Bound up tight, she had been able to ignore her bitter past. But now, something in her mind had given up; a threadbare knot had come undone, and everything tumbled out. Her chest became tight, and tears pricked the corners of her eyes. Her lip quivered, and she gave up trying to hold it all back. She began to sob.

Her bedroom door opened, and Crumpet stood there, watching, "Ms Pudding?" He enquired formally, "Are you unwell?"

Sylvia pushed passed him, shoving him back out of the room and closing the door. She rushed over and sat on the edge of Greta's bed.

"What's happened?" She cooed, "What's the matter?"

"I'm not as nice a person as I seem." Greta said, her bottom lip trembling. Sylvia's reassuring presence enabled Greta to calm herself a little, and to control her tears and sobs. Clive slunk up the bed and rubbed his cheeks on the back of Greta's shaking hands.

Sylvia didn't know what to do. She had never seen Greta upset. Angry, yes. But never like this, "I think you're lovely." Sylvia said, "Prickly, but lovely underneath it all."

Greta shook her head, "No. Underneath all the prickles, it's just more prickles, and ugliness, and nasty thoughts."

"What's got into you?" Sylvia was worried, "You're never like this. What's happened?"

"I had a nightmare."

"Oh is that all?"

"But not just any old bad dream. It's something that really happened, that I've worked very hard to forget." Greta's eyes were red, and tears had left wet tracks down her sunken cheeks.

"Greta?" Sylvia gently rubbed her friend's back, "Tell me about it."

"You'll hate me, when I tell you."

"I won't," Sylvia said, "Don't be silly."

"You will." Greta said, and a gasping sob escaped from her. She began to weep once more as she told her story.

*

Greta had spent weeks waiting on him, hand and foot. She had to, he was her husband, after all. Despite everything. He wheezed loudly every time he took a breath in, and his face was pinched in pain. Constant pain. She cleared away the plate of chips and gravy, barely nibbled, from the bedside table. It's all he wanted to eat these days. Yet he had no appetite. His cup of tea had gone cold too, and was untouched.

Pevril began to cough. It was a hacking, wheezing, wet series of explosions in his chest, forcing him to convulse. Greta stood and watched him for a long time.

"This is no way to live." She said.

"Don't worry," Pevril said, wiping phlegm from his lips, "There's no chance of me shuffling off just yet, and leaving you to your own devices." He said it with a neutral tone, and so Greta couldn't decipher if he was being kindly or cruel.

"The doctor's due again tomorrow morning." Greta said, if only for something to say. Their conversations were stunted, and limited to Pevril's medical needs.

"You think you'll get around to cleaning out my bed pan before then?" Pevril wheezed, an evil glint in his eye.

"I'll think about it." Greta said, matching his look.

"You enjoy this don't you?" Pevril sneered, "Me being bed-bound and at death's door."

"I wish you'd hurry up and knock." She sniped.

"Suppose you feel like you've the upper hand now?"

"Upper hand?"

"In this game of ours."

"Game?" Greta's eyes went wide, "Is that what you think this is?"

Pevril grinned, "It's what we made it."

"It's what you made it! I've played my part very well, I thank you. I've been the perfect wife!"

Pevril laughed, and caused himself another coughing fit. The explosions went off wetly deep inside his ribs, bringing a little blood up onto his teeth, "You're hilarious." He said, "Delusional."

Greta stared at him, any kindness she had felt for her ill husband evaporated, and she ground her dentures.

"You and me, we're very much alike. We're the perfect worst match in the history of marriages!"

"We are nothing alike!" Greta hissed, "You are cruel, and cowardly, and…" She stopped herself. It wouldn't do to berate a dying man. She turned and made to leave the room.

"And?" Pevril goaded.

Pausing at the door to his room, Greta sighed heavily and said, "I honestly wish you'd hurry up and die."

"There she is. There's that vinegary old onion-wife of mine." They stood there a while, eyes locked, daring one another to say more, to continue the argument, to escalate it, to shout and to scream and to not hold back. But they were both of them taut and rigid, neither would be the first to give.

Eventually Pevril shifted in the bed, tugged one of the pillows from behind his head, and offered it to Greta, "Go on then." He said.

"What?" Greta stared at the pillow, not understanding.

"Finish me off. Smother me. Win this game of marriage. Be the one to survive it."

Greta stared at the pillow for a long time, and her mind went blank.

*

"I killed him." Greta said as tears rolled down her cheeks, her breathing interrupted by sobs, "He was so ill, and I was so angry, it just made sense."

Sylvia didn't know whether to hug Greta, or call the police, "I don't understand."

"He offered me the pillow, and told me to smother him. He dared me. And I was so angry with him. I still am. I had bottled it all up, kept it hidden and ignored for so long." She took a deep breath, trying to calm herself, "I took it, and I pushed it over his face."

"Oh Greta!" Sylvia could think of nothing else to say.

"And he just lay there." Greta's sobs intensified, "He didn't struggle. He let me do it! And that made me even angrier. I wanted him to struggle, to fight back, to stop me. But he didn't. I killed him."

Sylvia made up her mind, and wrapped her arms around Greta, pulling her in for a hug. She buried the frail woman in her bosom, and stroked her back with one hand, "Oh Greta!" She said, "Oh dear, oh Greta!"

Greta clung to her friend, wetting the front of her dress with tears and snot, "I'm a horrible person." She said, her words broken into fragments by racked sobs. Clive watched the two women embrace, blinking slowly.

"You're not a horrible person," Sylvia said, struggling to find supportive words, "You might think you've done a horrible thing, but it sounds to me like he wanted to go. You helped to end his suffering. What you did was a kindness." Sylvia said the words, but wasn't entirely sure she believed them.

After a few minutes Greta's weeping subsided, and she released her grip on Sylvia's dress, "I need a cup of tea." She sniffed, wiping her eyes on her sleeve, and knocking her glasses askew.

From the corner of the room came a gentle squeak. It was the sound of a stiff metal joint moving. It was the sound of the tin soldier turning his head to watch the old women. He had heard it all, and something inside of him changed. What remained of Pevril Pudding shifted uncomfortably within its tin carapace.

"Be careful." He said, and ran away as soon as they laid eyes on him. He couldn't explain the warning. He didn't truly understand what he was warning them about. But he knew something was coming. Something dangerous. And he hid once again inside the mouse tunnels that laced the walls and floors of the Hospital.

"What does he mean, 'be careful'?" Sylvia pondered.

"He's threatening me. That's what he means. I'm to be careful, or he'll end my life the way I ended his. That's why he's back, like Angelica said,

I summoned him. It's my own shame. My own guilt. He won't stop until I'm dead."

Chapter Nine
Playthings On Parade

21st of December.

Over tea and toast, Sylvia told Crumpet what Greta had admitted the night before. He leaned against the kitchen worktop slowly chewing his buttery toast, listening quietly. Once more she seemed compelled to spill everything, against her better judgement. What she had been told was deeply private, and incredibly sensitive. Why could she not control her tongue around Crumpet?

"She's sound asleep now. I don't think we'll see her up until later, if at all, today." Sylvia said, and went to slurp her tea. Toast crumbs had fallen in it, and she picked them out before taking a gulp.

Crumpet looked up at her finally, swallowing the well-masticated mouthful, "She is certainly a very interesting woman." He said.

"Is that it?" Sylvia asked, "I tell you all that, and that's all you can say?"

Crumpet shrugged, "Honestly, I'm not surprised. But I am by no means familiar enough with her to offer any advice or words of comfort. She's your friend. Proceed how you think best." He rubbed his chin.

Sylvia sighed, holding her cup in both hands to warm them through, "That's just the thing; I don't know what I think. Pevril did sort-of deserve it, the old devil. But that's the kind of thing you say, not do. People say 'oh i'll kill him' but never really mean it, never really do it."

"But she did."

"Yes. She did."

Sylvia mulled it over for much of the day, served the single customer who came in to collect their mended teddy bear, and stewed. At the end of the day she flipped the sign around to say 'closed', turned off the Hospital lights, and took a plate of cheese and biscuits up to Greta.

She perched on the edge of the bed, and Greta hid beneath the duvet.

"You need to eat something." Sylvia said, "I'm not having you waste away up here like Miss Havisham, all morose and peculiar."

"What did you bring me?" Greta mumbled through the covers.

"Cheese and biscuits."

"Hardly a balanced meal."

Sylvia tugged the covers away from Greta's face, and waved the plate at her, "Sit up and eat up. Come on. Nurse Garland says so. Do as you're told."

"I Suppose your opinion of me has changed a bit." Greta said, reluctantly taking the plate and sitting up.

"I suppose it has." Sylvia nodded.

"I'll understand if you want to move out." Greta was meek, quiet, and nibbled on a bit of cheese. She seemed quite unlike her usual self.

"What's happened, Greta?" Sylvia probed, "You came home from shopping yesterday and something was off. I could tell. And then you wake up and tell me all that..." Sylvia sighed, "Something's the matter, and I wish you'd tell me what it was."

Greta shook her head, "I wish I knew. I feel like my head's a mess. I can't think straight. It's as if the neat and tidy little office in my head, where all the memories are kept, has been shaken up like a snow globe, and everything's gone all over the place."

Sylvia watched her friend for a long time. The Greta she knew was gone. In front of her was someone else. A stranger. Or rather, in front of her now was the true Greta, the one who had always been there, in disguise. Now that the mask had slipped, Sylvia had some decisions to make.

"I'm not one for making rash decisions." She said slowly, "Not any more. So I'm not going to be packing my bags just yet. But I have realised that I never really knew you, Greta Pudding. I suspect you hid a lot more from me than what you revealed last night."

Greta couldn't look Sylvia in the eye, "I don't deserve you as a friend."

"I'll be the judge of that, if you please." Sylvia heaved herself up from the bed, her knees clicking as she did, "Now eat up and stop moping. We've some conversations to have."

"Not tonight." Greta said, handing back the plate of cheese and biscuits, barely touched, "But tomorrow, I promise, ask me anything you want and I'll tell you the truth."

Sylvia nodded and left the room, leaving Greta still holding the plate of food.

Greta's attention was taken to her bedside table, where Little Miss Molly Radish sat staring at her. Had she been there this whole time? Maybe Sylvia had brought her in as a comforter. Hugging the dolly to her chest, Greta rolled over in bed and closed her eyes tight.

"Was Pevril a very bad man?" Asked Molly Radish

"Not to begin with." Greta said, then her eyes went wide and she sat bolt upright in bed, "Who's there?" She demanded.

"It's me, silly."

Greta looked down at the doll in her arms, as the porcelain head swivelled to look up at her, "Molly?"

"Surprise!" Molly giggled.

Sylvia raced back into Greta's room as soon as she heard her name called.

"What is it?" She asked, seeing Greta sat bolt upright in bed holding Little Miss Molly Radish at arms length.

"She spoke!" Greta said, eyeballing the dolly.

"Seems quiet now." Sylvia observed.

"Say something!" Greta demanded, shaking the doll, "Go on, say something! Speak!"

Sylvia took the doll from her friend.

"I'm not going mad." Greta said.

Little Miss Molly Radish was mute in Sylvia's hands, as she expected, "You might have dreamed it." She said.

Greta shook her head, "No. And I didn't imagine it either. I'm not doolally. That dolly spoke!" She pointed an accusing finger at the doll, a shaky finger.

"It wouldn't be the weirdest thing to have happened so far this Christmas, would it?"

Greta ground her dentures together, and her bed-flattened blue rinse trembled as she shook her head, "I can't get my thoughts in order." She ran her hands over her tired face, "Do me a favour, and keep Molly in the bird cage in the living room tonight?"

Sylvia raised an eyebrow, "If you insist."
"I do insist. Please."

Sylvia did as Greta asked, and locked Little Miss Molly Radish in the bird cage that had until a few days ago been Pevril's prison. Furious Crumpet watched her curiously.

"Don't ask." Sylvia said, before he had chance to ask any questions.

This duty done, Sylvia hurried to her bedroom and closed the door. She took up the broken hand mirror and tapped the glass.

"Angie?" She whispered, hoping that both Crumpet and Greta would not hear her, "Ange? Angelica?" She tapped the glass again, "I could really do with a bit of guidance." The reflection of her cousin failed to materialise. Sylvia sagged onto her bed, "Please."

Sylvia held the handle of the mirror in both hands, squeezing it, silently begging for the witch to reappear. When she failed to summon her, Sylvia felt suddenly very alone and isolated. True, she had Crumpet, but she didn't really know him very well. The haste with which she had agreed to moving him in played on her mind, and with her oldest friend entirely out of sorts, and behaving like never before, she felt like a tattered flag in a gate; blown every which way, and slowly into pieces.

She put the mirror down and sighed.

The bedroom door opened and Crumpet appeared, "*Cara mia*, are you ok?"

Sylvia nodded, "I think I'm going to get an early night and bury my nose in a book for a bit. You stay up and watch the tele-box."

Crumpet nodded a brief bow, and closed the door over.

At once, Sylvia opened the witchy casket and started leafing through the notebooks, "There has to be something amongst all this gubbins that can help me!"

22nd of December.

"Today is the day of closest conjunction." Said Little Miss Molly Radish quietly.

Crumpet held the puzzle box, his strange key, in both hands, "A few hours more, only." He said, "Be patient, oh Everything."

"Who are you talking to?" Sylvia said, poking her head into the living room. Late morning sunlight through the window cast Crumpet as a silhouette.

"Just myself."

"I'll be downstairs. I'm putting the kettle on and getting a load of bacon and eggs on the go."

"Delicious."

"But I need to have some private time with Greta this morning, so I'll bring yours up presently. Make yourself busy up here until I tell you it's all clear?"

Crumpet nodded, "I shall do."

Sylvia nodded to Molly Radish in the cage, "Get that down off the ceiling would you? Save me getting the ladder up from downstairs."

Crumpet obliged, passing the caged doll to Sylvia.

"Ta, lovey." She said, and bustled away.

*

The smell of breakfast drew Greta from her fortress of crocheted blankets and eiderdown pillows. She hobbled slowly down the steep stairs into the kitchen, and gratefully accepted the plate of crispy bacon and runny-yolked fried eggs. The cage, with Little Miss Molly Radish within, sat on the worktop by the kettle.

Sylvia plonked herself opposite her friend at the tiny kitchen table, and watched Greta bring the first mouthful to her lips before being unable to contain herself any longer, "I think we need to come clean, Greta Pudding." She blurted.

Greta froze, her mouth open, and her eyes flicked up to stare at Sylvia. A bit of egg fell off her fork and onto the collar of her dressing down.

"To the proper authorities." Sylvia said meaningfully.

Greta lowered her fork, and brushed the egg crumb away, "Do you think they'll send me to prison?"

Sylvia pushed a business card across the table. It was the card left by Miss Moss and Gildroy Silver; the business card for the Funeral Home For The Unusually Deceased, "I don't know much about prison, but doubt these folk deal much with living people who need incarcerating."

"The proper authorities?" Greta muttered, staring at the card, "That girl said something was coming, something dangerous, and that if anything came out of the hole in the skirting, that we should tell her." Her eyes flicked to Molly Radish, sat still and silent in her prison.

Sylvia boggled, casting her eyes to the doll on the worktop as well, "When was this?"

"Day before yesterday." Greta shrugged, "But I thought she was exaggerating. Fishing for business, or something. We've seen those ghost hunting shows on TV. It's all a sham."

"Oh Greta Pudding you daft old idiot." Sylvia slapped her palms onto the table top, "With everything that's happened, you ignored her warning?" Swivelling in her seat, she glared at Molly, and said quietly, "She doesn't look dangerous, does she?"

"No." Greta agreed, "But we know how appearances can deceive.

Sylvia turned back to Greta and said, "Yes indeed." With a meaningful sigh. She then produced a small notebook, "This is one of Angelica's books," She said, "I was going through them last night, and amongst all the stuff in code, the diary entries, and instructions on how to use mirrors to summon the dead, I found this." She opened the book and tapped a page.

Greta scanned the lines of slanted handwriting, and her mouth dropped open. She pulled the notebook closer, and adjusted her glasses, reading the passage again, and reading more. After a minute or two she slapped the book closed and grimaced gleefully, "I knew he was no good!"

Sylvia took the book back, "It's a unique name, so there's no way it's not about him."

"But how did she know him in the twenties? He doesn't look anywhere near old enough."

Sylvia shrugged, "Magic. Maybe? I don't know. But Angelica Tiffin knew Furious Crumpet in the twenties, and he was up to some right shady business."

"I'd bet you any money he's still up to the same shady business in my Toy Hospital!"

Sylvia had puppy eyes, "And I brought him into our lives. I'm sorry Greta. I should have listened to you."

Greta and Sylvia held hands over the formica table-top.

"You don't need to apologise, Sylv." Greta squeezed her friend's hand, "But what are we to do? How are we supposed to find out what he's up to?"

Sylvia sighed heavily, "Tie him up and whack him with socks full of stinky kippers until he tells us everything?"

Greta snorted with laughter. Sylvia grinned, and the two of them chuckled.

"Don't think all this carry-on gets you off the hook, however." Sylvia wagged a finger at Greta, "We still need to have some serious conversations. But let's prioritise, eh?"

Greta nodded, "One problem at a time. Let's get Frisky Crinoline out of our house."

"Flatulent Conker." Sylvia snorted.

"Festering Crumble." Greta chortled.

Sylvia shook her head, "He really has got a very stupid name, hasn't he?"

"I'll let my parents know you think so." Said Crumpet, beginning to descend the stairs.

Greta stood up, "Earwigging, were you?"

Crumpet smiled his half-smile, "Of course."

"You've some explaining to do." Greta said, "Who are you really? You can drop this Cesar Romero lookalike act. There's something otherwise about you. I've known it since I first clapped eyes on you."

He tossed the puzzle box in the air and caught it, "You really would have been quite a formidable witch, had you ever had training."

Sylvia and Greta looked at each other.

"What?" Sylvia said.

"Didn't she tell you?" He cocked an eyebrow, "She's a witch."

Greta's mouth hung open, "No I'm not."

Crumpet brushed a hand over Sylvia's cheek.

"*Bella rabbia.*" He cooed, "Greta is a deceiver, and you don't really know her at all, do you?"

"No." Sylvia blinked, and turned to Greta, scowling, "He's right. You've spent your whole life telling fibs and hiding the truth." As she spoke, she became more and more furious, "You're a hypocrite, a miserable old goat, never letting me do what I want. What a controlling old hag you are."

"Sylv?" Greta was confused, why had her friend suddenly turned on her?

"Who are you, Greta Pudding? Who are you really?" Sylvia spat.

"Sylvia, he's done something to you." Greta said, it was the only possible explanation.

"Don't try deflecting my attention. You're a murderess. How could I ever trust you?"

Greta's mouth flapped as she searched for words, "I may well be those things, but Crumpet is the one we should be haranguing!" She jabbed a finger in his direction. He was laughing at her, and she saw red, and she lost control. How dare he laugh at her! She wasn't some pathetic old woman. She wasn't there for some man's amusement. She strode forward quickly and slapped him hard across the face. The shock sent him reeling and for a moment, just a moment, Greta saw that he had horns. When he straightened up and faced her again the horns were gone, and so was his smile.

"As amusing as all this is," Said a girlish voice from the counter-top, "The time has come."

The slap had not only shocked Crumpet, but had broken whatever hold he had over Sylvia, "Oh Greta!" She said, and hugged her friend tightly.

Molly Radish waved at the three of them, "If you could let me out, I'd be very grateful."

Sylvia and Greta stared at Little Miss Molly Radish.

"I knew I wasn't going doolally." Greta said.

"How can you talk?" Sylvia asked, "Are you a ghost?"

Molly giggled, "In a manner of speaking."

Crumpet unlatched the cage door, and Molly stepped stiffly out, "Servant, the key." She commanded.

Crumpet bowed and produced the puzzle box.

"That's a key?" Greta wondered.

"Servant?" Sylvia knitted her brow in confusion, "Are you a servant to a talking dolly?"

Crumpet wound the handle on the puzzle box. With each rotation it went ding! louder and louder, until finally the box sprang open. Sylvia and Greta stepped back from it automatically, raising their arms to shield their faces. But nothing happened. Four pairs of eyes stared at the open puzzle box.

"It's empty?" Greta relaxed, "I was sure it was going to explode or something."

"Me too." Sylvia agreed.

Carrying the open puzzle box with extreme care and reverence, Crumpet made his way through the kitchen and into the front of the Toy Hospital. As he moved further forward, the puzzle box began to change shape. It began to twist and distort, and from deep within came a sickly green light.

"Oh I don't like the look of that." Greta muttered.

Dashing to the phone by the counter, Sylvia began dialling a number.

"It won't make a difference if you make that call or not." Said Molly Radish, in her high pitched child-like voice, "No one can stop me."

Crumpet put the puzzle box down and marched towards the old ladies. Greta put herself in his path, "If you lay one hand on my friend I'll box your ears!"

The phone was answered, and Sylvia began talking quickly, "We need your help!"

Crumpet pushed Greta out of the way, but the old woman clung onto his clothes, knocking him off balance.

"The Toy Hospital." Sylvia gabbled, "There's a talking dolly from the hole. Furious Crumpet's her minion! Please come quickly!"

Despite Greta hanging off of him, Crumpet reached Sylvia easily and tore the receiver from her hand. In three quick motions he had smashed it into pieces on the counter top.

Greta fell from him, and took Sylvia's hands in hers, "Come on, let's get out of here."

They stumbled towards the front door, but Molly Radish stood in their way, "Don't you want to stay and play?" She giggled.

"I'll kick you out of the way if I have to!" Greta threatened.

Ding!

The puzzle box, rested on the edge of the display table in the middle of the Hospital, had twisted into a strange hourglass shape, inside of which green light convulsed, spinning around glass beads and silver wire. As it made a ding, it released a flair of bright oily light into the room.

This brought the old women up short, and they turned to stare at it, "What's it doing?" Sylvia asked.

"What a key is supposed to do." Crumpet said, "It's opening a door."

Little Miss Molly Radish began to laugh. It was a high pitched, childish giggle, that continued longer than it should have, shifting, modulating, cracking. The laugh broke and became a hyena cackle, shrill and bestial.

Greta and Sylvia clung to each other as the floor beneath their slippered feet began to tremble.

An aurora borealis of rippling shades of teal and indigo spilled like ink into the air from the glowing, twisting key. Crumpet opened the cupboard door, and stepped back. The flowing light then spiralled, twisted, and began to drain into the cupboard like water down a plug hole.

"I don't like the look of this." Sylvia said.

"I'm sorry." Greta said, "I'm sorry for everything, for being a prickly old bitch, for-"

The open cupboard bulged, strained, and groaned. The walls of the Hospital creaked and shook, as plaster began to cascade from above. Dark cracks split across the walls, ceiling, and floor; Dark cracks more like shadows than breaks in plaster or board.

Greta and Sylvia clutched each other tightly as the floor began to quake. The toys were shaken about, and began to tumble from their shelves, climbing over one another, standing on plush, wooden, and plastic legs, coming alive! A doll's house opened, and the wooden peg dollies hopped out. Carved wooden animals began to prowl across the floor. A music box opened, playing a tinny nutcracker suite, as a plastic ballerina twirled en pointe inside. Hanging on string from the ceiling, a wooden biplane began to spin and struggled to be free. The rocking horse in the window whinnied, and see-sawed violently back and forth.

Molly laughed harder and harder, hopping from one leg to another excitedly as the pulsing of the sickly light accelerated. The key flared once more, releasing flickering energy and showering the room with sparks. The Christmas lights went out as the plastic tree toppled over. The toys began to dance, and fight, and bundle together, rolling about in thrusting clumps. With a grinding wail, the cupboard yawned wide, and the Toy Hospital was gone.

*

Being the day before Christmas Eve, the snowy streets of Manchester were already full of intrepid last-minute shoppers. The sky was blue and clear, and a brisk wind snatched at scarfs, and made noses red. Minute by minute however, the sky darkened, as thick clouds began to form.

"Did that just move?" Asked a small boy, peering into a shop window. He had been taken out to help his mother shop for his father's Christmas present, and had naturally been drawn away from the drudgery of hardware and gardening shops to a window display full of colourful toys. A stack of the latest Beanie Babies sat alongside Barbies, etch-a-sketches, and the usual array of toy cars, teddies, and assorted inaccurate plastic animals.

His mother didn't look, as her attention was taken by the sky, "It's incredibly rare to see the aurora borealis this far south!" She said, watching as blue and green light swirled across the sky. The lights pulsed beneath the thickening clouds.

"Looks like a storm is on the way." She said, "We should probably find a cafe to wait it out in."

"It definitely moved. Look, mummy!" The boy tugged on his mother's sleeve urgently.

"What did?" His mother shifted her attention to the shop window and gasped. The Barbie and Ken dolls were moving about, enacting some very adult activities.

"Oh my!" She said, instinctively covering her son's eyes.

But it wasn't just the plastic dolls that had seemingly come to life. The shop beyond heaved with activity as toys broke free of their plastic and cardboard prisons. Inside, someone screamed, and someone else fell over their own feet as they ran from the shop in fright. Something came hurtling through the air at the shop window, shattering it. Mother and son screamed as shards of glass fell all around them.

Then came the cavalcade of toys. They leaped and hopped and stamped out of the broken pane and through the open door into the snow. Shouts and screams went off near and far, as similar scenes repeated again and again. The mother pulled her son to her, and edged away up the street. She tripped on the snow-concealed curb and fell. Around them the toys jeered and sneered, cartwheeled and pranced.

The stream of thrusting, lolloping, slinking playthings made their way across the street, where they joined another roiling swarm of toys spilling from the shattered window of a Woolworths.

Marching hugger-mugger off into the back streets of Manchester went the toys, scattering terrified and screaming shoppers in all directions. The clouds darkened further, as the sickly-green aurora borealis pulsed and shimmered across Manchester's rooftops.

Similar scenes repeated again and again across the city, and soon all intrepid festive shoppers gave up on their endeavours, and fled or hid to watch the parading playthings.

The streams of toys joined, and became rivers, which joined others, and became a tide. They rolled and bounced and leaped and cartwheeled and jumped towards the origin of their peculiar summoning; the Toy Hospital, from the roof of which erupted the iridescent lights of the aurora.

The door stood open, and the interior was impenetrably dark. Into this blackness fell the endless flow of animated toys.

*

Greta realised she had been screaming. The end of her scream echoed around the cavern they now found themselves in. Sylvia was trembling.

"What happened?" Greta asked, getting a hold of herself, "Where are we?"

The Hospital had opened like a pop-up book, split wide, changed, and been altered by shifting layers of card and paper scenes. What had once been their cosy, albeit slightly rundown Hospital, was now a vast underground cavern, lit by sparkling threads of light that dangled from the distant roof.

"We are in your Toy Hospital." Said Furious Crumpet, "We have simply blurred the lines between this world, and what exists outside of it."

"Outside of the world?" Sylvia's mouth hung open, "What are you talking about?"

"Welcome to what certain occult circles refer to as the Abject Void." Crumpet gestured grandly.

"Doesn't look like a void to me." Greta sniped.

"Not very voidy at all." Sylvia chimed in quietly.

"Looks like Wookey Hole."

Crumpet tutted, "It's just a fancy name."

The toys of the Hospital were all around them, and all of them alive. They jibbered and jabbered in nonsense verse, danced about, and made very merry with one another.

"Why are we here?" Greta asked, turning to Little Miss Molly Radish, who stood beside the open Toy Hospital door; the one thing that remained of their home. Through the door there was nothing but darkness.

The doll giggled, "There's little joy in victory if it is unobserved. You're my audience! And if I'm hungry later, maybe my dinner too."

Sylvia gulped, "I don't think I want to be a dolly's dinner."

"You stop that!" Greta swiped at a Barbie trying to put her hand up a squirming puppet.

"Yank my stuffing!" Cried the puppet, its flimsy jaws flapping wide.

The cavorting toys laughed and yelled in high, warbling voices; revelling in their role of mischievous imps.

"I always knew you were some kind of a ne'er-do well." Greta brandished one of her gnarled fingers at Crumpet, "But what exactly are you? You're no regular man, that's for sure."

Crumpet grinned with one side of his mouth, "In your language the name of my people would translate as We Walk In Midnight." Greta and Sylvia stared at him blankly. "Colloquially, though, I suppose 'demon' will suffice. *Verità!*"

He shook his head, and then his body, like a dog shakes water from its coat. When the shaking was done, Furious Crumpet looked very different. Where there had been polished shoes, now there were cloven hooves. Where there had been manicured nails, now there were claws, and where there had been a devilishly handsome face, now there was the head of a goat. His pelt was black and grey, and his eyes blazed orange. Two sets of horns decorated his head, a pair that stuck up in the air, and another pair that curled around his drooping velvet ears.

Sylvia gasped, a hand to her mouth.

"You kissed that." Greta said.

"And the rest." Sylvia gagged slightly at the thought of his bleating face bearing down upon her in the night, the farmyard stench, the coarse bristling hair of his chin and neck and chest, "I feel sick."

Molly regarded the old women with unblinking glass eyes, "We must be on our way."

"On our way?" Sylvia feared the worst, "To where?"

Molly pointed behind them, to where the cupboard had once been, where now a dark tunnel extended, downward into the red earth, "To what remains of me."

Crumpet held out a long clawed hand, gesturing for the women to lead the way, "Hurry now, we mustn't dillydally."

"I absolutely refuse to go anywhere unless you tell me exactly what's going on!" Greta folded her arms.

The ground began to shake. An earthquake?

"What now?" Sylvia whimpered.

No, not an earthquake. Something else. Something growing nearer. From behind them, from the dark opening of the Hospital door, a strange sound began. It was a burbling, chittering sound, like a million angry voices. In the faint light of the cavern it was hard to tell, but something was emerging from that dark aperture. Like a cresting wave breaking upon rocks, foaming and rolling a thousand toys cascaded over them from the darkness. The play-things of Manchester erupted across the cavern, spilling in all directions. It was upon the old women in a moment, snatching their feet from under them, picking them up, and carrying them aloft, as Crumpet and Molly laughed. Down the tunnel they all went, the screams of Sylvia echoing on the walls, and Greta's defiant shouts of protest were made unintelligible in the burble of chattering, giggling toys.

Along dark passages, and over bridges the toys carried their four passengers. Molly and Crumpet seemed quite content, held aloft by enormous cuddly bears and monkeys, while Sylvia and Greta were tumbled about, head over feet again and again, passed from one group of toys to another. The caverns stretched on and on, each new opening more jagged and twisted than the last. It was a labyrinth, marked by canyons, derelict and crumbling walls, and an ever-growing stench of rotting meat.

Eventually they were deposited in a wide circular space. This cavern had a high arched ceiling, marked by cracks, and fallen pillars lay like the bones of a long-dead leviathan.

The tide of toys slowly dwindled, and Greta and Sylvia fought to catch their breath. They were close to being buried by the sea of toys, but Crumpet grabbed them by the wrist and pulled them to the surface.

"Greta?" Sylvia grabbed at her friend, "Are you hurt?"

"Just bruised, I think." Greta said, struggling to stand on her own, "Ouch! My hip." She leaned on Sylvia for support, "Think I've pulled something."

"Where are we now?" Sylvia asked, looking around.

In the centre of the cavern, illuminated by a shaft of pale light lay a corpse. At least, it might have been a corpse. There was blackened, charred flesh, exposed bone, and blood dark as tar in a pool around it, and it was enormous.

Greta gagged at the smell, "What is that?" There was no clear head, the limbs were all different, and oddly placed.

"It was everything. And it was nothing. A fragment of a wondrous whole." Little Miss Molly Radish said conversationally, like she was talking perfect sense, "It is all that remains of me. The real me. The physical me."

"You're the ghost of that thing, trapped in a toy?" Greta asked.

"Putting it very simply," Furious strode between the women and the dolly, "Yes. And it's time to rejoin these pieces."

"What are you, though, truly?" Greta asked Molly, "Your body there is… well it's weird. Never seen anything like it. You're not just a regular dead person, not some kind of Walking In Midnight demon either, I'd wager."

The toys had dispersed around the cavern, exploring, playing games, miming fornication.

Molly waddled slowly towards the corpse, "I existed before there was death, and before demons, before dinosaurs, and stars, and dust. And I intend to reclaim all that once was; a glorious Nothing. My beautiful self, and nothing more. This universe is so noisy. It's about time I put a stop to it."

"Put a stop... to the universe!?" Greta shrieked, "but you can't! That's where we live!"

"Not for long." Smirked Little Miss Molly Radish.

Sylvia turned to Crumpet, "And what do you get out of all this? Hmm? Once everything is destroyed?"

"I'm a mercenary. I do what pays well. And between you and me, my benefactors have grander plans than annihilation."

Greta and Sylvia boggled, "Who are these benefactors of yours?"

Crumpet tapped his nose conspiratorially.

"That would be telling."

Molly turned to them, "It's rude to whisper." She giggled, "And I'm not destroying everything, I'm reclaiming. This world, this galaxy, this universe, and all the realms that sit alongside came from me, were a part of me."

Crumpet squinted at Molly, evidently receiving new information.

"What are you on about?" Greta snapped, "How can the world have come from you?"

"I was alone. I was everything. I was all that there was. I wanted company, I wanted to no longer be alone. And so I tried to make another of me, but I failed. I died, ish. I... dispersed, in the biggest explosion in all of history."

"The big bang?" Sylvia muttered, "You created the big bag?"

Molly rubbed her porcelain hands together, "Greta Pudding, your mind and your home fed me. Such delicious sorrow, with a drizzle of joy, and the seasoning that came with every lost and loved toy that came to you. I was much diminished, and barely aware, but I gained enough strength to reach into your mind and summon a temporary form." Molly curtseyed, "I think it suits me rather well."

"Were you always in my dolly, ever since I was a child?" Greta asked, bereft.

Molly shook her head, "I plucked this form from your memories. And I quite like it. Shame it will soon be obsolete." The doll seemed to become suddenly angry, looking around the vast room, "Where is the horned one?"

Furious Crumpet was nowhere to be seen.

Chapter Ten
Just Desserts

Furious Crumpet was truly only in service to one being; Himself. He hadn't survived so long only to be duped into becoming manservant to the apocalypse.

He knew when to cut his losses and run.

His cloven hooves tapped loudly on the stone and clay and slate floors of the tunnels and passages of the Abject Void. There was someone he needed to have some serious words with.

"The goats came marching, one by one…" Someone sang. The voice echoed from a thousand directions.

Crumpet stopped and spun about. Who else was here? There should be no one save those he brought with him.

"…hurrah, hurrah!" Sang the disembodied voice.

It took a moment for Crumpet to recognise the singer, and he narrowed his orange eyes scanning the nooks and crevices for the tin soldier.

"Come out, come out wherever you are." Crumpet sang into the dark.

A stone bounced off of his head, and he spun about, his eyes flicking to and fro, trying to identify its origin. Another stone hit him, from another direction. Crumpet spun around again, but once more could not identify from where it came.

Something darted between the rocks beside him, and Crumpet leaped towards the movement. It was a cat! A black, one-eyed cat, on the back of which rode the tin soldier! He launched a pebble at Crumpet's face as he was carried away, and it struck the goat-headed man between the eyes. He snarled, a strange bleating sound, and galloped after the cat and its rider.

*

Molly Radish shook her curly ginger hair, "The conjunction is upon us!"

The light that shone on the giant mangled corpse strewn across the centre of the room brightened. Greta could see no source, but it poured like liquid from the very air, picking out every grotesque detail of the vast decayed thing.

Little Miss Molly Radish walked slowly towards the hulking cadaver. Her painted shoes were soon splashing daintily through thick gloopy pools of dark blood, then miscellaneous viscera, which she bent down to scoop up with her stiff porcelain fingers. These tatters of rotten flesh she smeared over herself, her face, her hair, her pretty little frock.

"Disgusting." Greta grimaced, yet found that she couldn't take her eyes off of the vile spectacle.

Molly clambered over a mouldy tentacle, then over fingers that sprouted like cactus spines from a limb thick as a tree trunk.

"What will happen when you're in your body?" Sylvia asked, calling loudly to be heard over the jibbering toys.

"It's a surprise." Molly giggled, not pausing her progress.

Step by tiny step she waded deeper into the debris, until finally she was pulling herself up a slope of sloughing skin by her stiff fingers.

"She's headed for the middle, look," Greta said, "Where you can see its ribs poking out."

And sure enough, she was. Molly Radish paused at the edge of the open wound in the chest of the mountainous beast, and looked down, looked into the glistening entrails of her former body. There was movement there; Writhing and pulsing flesh, still pink and red and alive! Molly Radish held out her arms, and jumped into the vast chest cavity.

"Weeeee!" She cried out.

Greta and Sylvia heard her land with a wet thud several seconds later.

"What happens now?" Sylvia wondered.

"I dread to think." Greta said, edging ever so slightly closer to her friend.

"Why's it so quiet all of a sudden?"

Sylvia and Greta turned slowly about. The toys had all fallen silent, and stood still. Then, as one, they turned to face the centre of the chamber. This coincided with a new sound beginning. A wet sound, a slithering sound; the oozing, pulsing, thrusting sound of flesh knitting together with flesh on a massive scale.

The corpse began to move, to shift, to pull itself together. Broken arms, distorted legs, and writhing tentacles flexed, awkwardly scooping the masses of disgorged entrails back into itself. When this task was mostly complete, it pushed against the floor, beginning to heave itself up. As it rose slowly into a sitting position, Greta and Sylvia clung to each other and hurried behind a fallen pillar to hide. A mis-matched collection of eyes blinked and dilated, scanning the ground.

A mouth opened, and the beast roared. The air visibly trembled at the sound, and Greta and Sylvia clamped their hands over their ears. The roar ended, and behind it, buried within the deafening silence that followed, they could just make out the sound of Molly Radish giggling.

The toys, motionless and staring, now began to move. They rolled, and strolled, and skipped, and loped towards the unspeakable thing into which Molly had dived. Sylvia slapped Greta on the arm, astonished at what she was seeing.

"Look!" She pointed, unable to get the right words out, "What're they doing?"

The toys were piling up against the skin and dangling entrails of the thing. They climbed over one another, burrowing into its flesh, filling up the gaps in its body, crawling, clawing their way desperately into becoming one with their master; the being that accidentally began the universe.

As the bodies and forms of the millions of toys strengthened the Everything, it finally stood at its full height, stretched its multitudinous and mismatched arms, and let loose a triumphant wail.

"Shite." Said Greta, "We're done for."

*

Crumpet stalked slowly around a corner, his black ears twitching, waiting for another verse to lead him to the tin soldier. He rubbed his sore head. He had been subject to several barrages of stones and pebbles from the suddenly appearing and disappearing tin soldier on his feline steed. One sharp stone had caused a cut on his nose, and a tiny bead of red blood hung there.

His hooves tapped quietly on the hard slate flooring. The labyrinth of the Abject Void twisted and turned, each new passage different from the one before. He arrived at a spiral staircase, crumbling and slumped. It ran up through a crack in the jagged ceiling. A few grains of dust fell from the top of the stairs as Crumpet approached. He listened, his orange eyes wide. Where was that pesky little toy?

The ground shook, as something distant roared. The sound echoed through the passages of the Void, and Crumpet flinched at the shock of it breaking the silence. Deciding to abandon his search for the possessed toy, he returned to his mission of escape. There would be no use in getting utterly lost in the Void hunting for a pebble-chucking ghost, no matter how annoying it was. His sense of self-preservation was strong, and he trotted away.

At the top of the stairs Clive padded silently away from one patch of darkness to another, Pevril on his back wobbling and bobbling about.

*

The toys, all of them, had become one with the Everything. In adding their bulk to it, it seemed to strengthen, to grow, to solidify, and energise. It moved ponderously, becoming accustomed once more to manoeuvring its long-dormant bulk.

Greta and Sylvia watched from their hiding place, seemingly forgotten by the revivified eldritch terror. They were forced to the very edges of the room, into a crack in the cavern wall. The enormous feet and hooves and claws of the Everything had stamped about, shattering the fallen pillars, cracking the ground, and causing the whole place to quake.

"We need to get out of here or we'll be squashed flat." Sylvia said, peering out of their snug crevice.

Greta, smothered somewhat by her friend's bosom, gasped for breath, "I don't much fancy being a pancake."

Sylvia pointed across the cavern, "We need to make it back up that passage. That's the way we came in."

Holding hands to shore up their bravery, the two women edged from the nook. They tried to keep to what appeared to be the back of the Everything, so that its many rolling eyes wouldn't catch sight of them.

One of its tails whipped dangerously close, causing a huge gust of air to knock them sideways. Greta cried out as her painful hip collided with a sharp stone.

The Everything, drawn by the sound, turned and smiled. Its uneven mouth of peculiar teeth opened wide, drool beading at its corners, and reached one of its arms towards them.

Sylvia tried to pull Greta up as the enormous hand drew closer, it was made of cricket bats and toy cars, woven all throughout with blue and pink veins.

"Miss Molly was a dolly who was sick, sick, sick!" Sang Pevril, as Clive the cat bolted from somewhere close by. The cat flew at the approaching hand, claws extended, hissing. It did nothing. The Everything didn't flinch, but it was distracted. This gave Sylvia enough time to drag Greta onto her feet, and the two of them stumbled away.

"It's Pevril and Clive!" Sylvia gasped, "What are they doing here?"

Greta winced as they reached a tumble of fallen masonry and collapsed against it, "They're in league with that beastie!" Greta gasped.

The Everything swatted at Clive and Pevril, but its movements were too slow, too ponderous. Clive darted along the monster's arm, across a shoulder and down its back before landing elegantly on the floor and racing to Greta and Sylvia's side.

"Turn around." Pevril said, and Clive darted away.

Greta turned, and noticed another crevice in the cavern wall. Supported one another, they made their way into the narrow space.

The Everything shook its malformed head, and something like words began to emerge from its throat, "You are but mites and gnats. I am the origin of all. I am the Everything. I am Galthorym! And I shall be free!"

It turned slowly, and moved towards the passage through which the group had entered the cavern. It ducked down low to the ground, and crawled in. The passage was too small for its bulk, and so it squeezed itself, changed its shape, like an octopus, thrusting broken and twisting limbs into an aperture that should have been impossible to traverse.

Greta and Sylvia watched, agog, as the first of its arms, and most of its head disappeared into the passage.

"It's like watching toothpaste going back into the tube." Sylvia said.

Clive padded in circles at their feet, rubbing his head on their ankles. Pevril clung to the fur of the cat's neck, seemingly steering it.

"One, two, buckle my shoe." Pevril sang, "Three, four, shut the door."

Greta and Sylvia exchanged puzzled glances, "What is he on about?" Greta scowled.

Clive trotted off into the darkness of the crevice in which they hid, and as Greta's eyes adjusted to the dim light, she saw that it was a gently curving passage.

"I think he wants us to follow him." Sylvia said, and took the lead, helping Greta to hobble along as best she could in the tight space.

Greta took a quick look over her shoulder into the vast cavern, where the Everything was slowly pushing its body parts through the passage opening.

"This better be a shortcut," She said, "Or we're buggered."

As they made their way as fast as they could along the passage, they knew they were rising. They could tell by the gentle incline beneath their feet that with each twist and curl, they were drawing nearer and nearer to the surface. Or whatever constituted the surface in this inexplicable maze. Sylvia wore her thoughtful face, and it made Greta curious.

"Penny for them?" She enquired.

"Hmm?" Sylvia was drawn from her reverie, and smiled sidelong at her friend, "Call it a witch's intuition!" She smiled.

"But you're not a witch."

"I might be." Sylvia huffed.

"Go on then, what?"

"You were a bit off, I think, about Pevril. Yes he's back because of how guilty you feel, and the shame, and all that. But I don't think him killing you is the end goal." Sylvia was having a revelation, "I think, and don't dismiss this as silliness; I think you have to forgive yourself."

Greta scowled, "That doesn't sound right."

"Think about the prophecy!" Sylvia said, "The tin soldier in the troll's castle rescues the old woman. In the end the tin soldier turns back into the man, and he and his wife live happily ever after. It's not a sad story. It has a happy ending!"

Greta shook her head, "I wouldn't put much stock in witchy fables if I were you." But she couldn't deny the end of the story was preferable to death by nursery rhyme, or being stamped on by a huge beastie from before time.

"I may not be a witch," Sylvia said, "But if what Angelica suggested is true, and that you somehow conjured him from your guilt and shame, then what if..." She paused to catch her breath, "What if you also conjured him with a little bit of love and bravery?"

Greta snorted, "Not likely."

But as they hobbled onward, she couldn't help but wonder, watching the tin soldier wobble back and forth on Clive's back. Maybe a little bit of the young Pevril was in there, the Pevril she remembered from their early romance. The silly soldier boy, the daft romantic, the troubled dreamer; could that Pevril be in there too?

The passage opened out into a cavern. The same glittery-ceilinged cavern they first found themselves in, and there in the centre was the Toy Hospital door, still open and with nothing but blackness beyond.

Clive trotted out into the cavern, and Pevril sang, "One, two, buckle my shoe. Three, four, shut the door!"

Sylvia checked to see if the coast was clear.

"There's just us." She said.

The two of them hurried to the Toy Hospital door, and there they paused, staring into the blackness beyond the threshold. As they stared into it, they realised that it wasn't simply empty darkness, it was a swirling spiral of greys and blacks, inky and interwoven.

"It's like a moving magic-eye picture." Sylvia said, going cross-eyed, and having to look away, "It's making my head spin."

"Now what?" Greta wondered, "Close the door? Do we have to close the door?" This she addressed to Pevril, riding about on Clive, watching them.

"If we close the door, it might seal off this void place, trap Molly and her horrible Frankenstein body here." Sylvia thought out loud.

"With us on this side of it, surely we'll be trapped here too?" Greta worried. She had reached out towards the door handle, but froze.

"I don't think I'd like being trapped here with that thing." Sylvia shook her head.

"No. Me neither." Greta agreed.

A nasty squelching, crunching, scraping sound echoed around the cavern. The Everything was drawing close up the passage.

"So we have to go through the doorway, and close it behind us." Sylvia said, "And we have to do it quick."

A giant malformed hand appeared from the mouth of the passage, its nails digging into the hard ground. The muscles behind the hand went taught, as the Everything pulled itself slowly into the glittering cavern.

Greta ground her dentures together, as she stepped towards the doorway, then she spun around, "No!" She said loudly, "We can't go yet."

"What?" Sylvia's mouth gaped, "Why not?"

Another hand, this one clawed, and then a tentacle emerged from the mouth of the passage. Each limb, each digit, each part of the great beast woven throughout with the toys of Manchester.

"I've spent most of my life looking after them, mending them, caring for them." Greta said, pushing her glasses up her narrow nose, and letting go of Sylvia, standing on her own, "I'm not about to abandon them now."

"What are you talking about?" Sylvia pleaded, "It's the end of the world! We have to get a wriggle on!"

"No." Greta said, "There must be something we can do!" And then an idea came to her. Crumpet had said she was a witch, though he was trying to set Sylvia against her at the time, it made her wonder. Maybe that was true? She had summoned the ghost of her dead husband after all. That seemed quite a witchy thing to have done.

"You've made all those wonderful toys monstrous." Greta said to the slowly approaching limbs of the Everything, "Shame on you."

"Greta!" Sylvia grabbed her friend's sleeve and tried to pull her towards the door.

If she was able to summon Pevril from beyond the veil, and by extension the flies, and spiders, and birds, and cats that he had himself summoned, then perhaps she was powerful enough to command the toys to abandon Molly Radish. Greta closed her eyes and clenched her fists, concentrating her thoughts. She didn't quite know what to do, and so made up a little spell.

"Toys of my fair Manchester, take back the power stole from yer. The Everything is nought but gristle, and to the end of time it can bloody well whistle." She didn't know where it came from, but it rhymed, and it sounded like it should do something.

The Everything laughed. It was a nasty, wet, gnashing, crunching sound, devoid of hilarity and full of spite.

"What are you trying to do?" Sylvia shouted over the din of its laughter.

"I'm trying to save the toys!" She yelled back, staring dead ahead at the flailing limbs, as more body parts began to erupt wetly into the cavern.

The laughter was maddening. Seeing red, incensed by the beast's derisive cackle, Greta screamed, "I command you to release those beautiful toys!" A tear pricked her eye, and her voice trembled with emotion.

From the mouth of the passage the vast maw of the Everything erupted, all teeth and tongues and spit. With the swipe of one hand, the Everything scooped up Greta Pudding and swallowed her whole.

"Greta!" Sylvia screamed, and fell to her knees. In a flash, Clive, with Pevril on his back, dashed forward, bounding over rocks and flailing limbs, following Greta down the creature's throat.

"Sylvia?" Furious Crumpet tumbled from a high crevice, landing awkwardly on one knee, "We need to get out of here."

Sylvia tore her gaze from the smacking lips of the Everything, and scowled deeply at the goat-headed man, "You're not going anywhere." She said grimly, standing, and cracking her knuckles,

"I'm not a violent woman. But for you I might make an exception."

*

Greta Pudding landed in a knee-deep puddle. She was splashed all over with the various liquids of the Everything's innards, and it stunk. She groaned in pain, and held a hand to her hip. It felt a little more than bruised. She was in some kind of cavity within the thing's chest. The walls around her flexed and rippled as the body beyond pushed and pulled itself into the doorway cavern. Blue and purple veins laced the wet sides of this space, and here and there parts of toys could be seen embedded in the flesh. A teddy's face and button eyes here, a tangle of yo-yo's there. In this dark place she could see, yet there was no light.

"I brought you here to bear witness, not to interfere." Said Little Miss Molly Radish. She was half-embedded in the wall, veins and nerve tissues leaching onto her porcelain body.

Greta refused to appear weak in front of anyone, least of all this deplorable abomination. She stood, painfully, and addressed the doll.

"Little Miss Molly Radish, I'm very disappointed in you."

The doll laughed, and black oil oozed from between her red painted lips.

"And I order you to release your hold on all these poor toys."

"All matter in your universe is mine, came from me, and will be a part of me again. Time, space, the abutting realms, all of it is me! I am simply reclaiming what I lost, so long ago. Surely you cannot deny me? I merely want to live!"

"At the expense of... everything!"

"I *am* Everything!" Molly screamed.

"Not any more." Greta shook her head, "And if I have anything to do with it, never again."

Molly quaked with anger, "You are within me already, old woman. Soon your atoms will break apart and merge with mine, and you will be home. There is nothing you can do."

Greta tried to move, but the soles of her shoes seemed stuck in place.

"It is happening already." Molly sneered.

Something fell - splop - into the wetness beside Greta, splashing her with more stinky stuff.

Clive yowled at being wet, and leaped to a dryer level. Pevril sang, as the cat shook itself dry.

"Miss Molly was a dolly who was sick, sick, sick..."

Tendrils of flesh broke off from the walls, and lashed out at the cat and the toy. But all of them missed their target, as Clive was too quick, too nimble to be caught.

"I command you, toys, to be free! I am Greta Pudding, and I loved you, I cared for you. Well, some of you, anyhow. Now, obey me!" Ignored by Molly now that the distraction of Clive and Pevril had arrived, she was given time to think. She watched the cat and the tin soldier dart about, leaping, clawing, dancing.

"Miss Molly was a dolly..." Pevril leaped from Clive's back at Molly Radish, taking hold of her dirty porcelain face, "...and her head popped off!" He pulled with all his might, and off flew the doll's head. Greta caught it, and couldn't help but laugh. Everything was so ridiculous, so desperate, so confounding, she could do nothing but laugh. It was a miraculous release of tension, and it instantly cleared her head.

"Oh my!" She realised, "I've been going about this all wrong."

She ran her thumb over Molly's face, and smiled.

"What are you grinning for, hag?" Molly's voice seemed to come from the air, and no longer from the dolly.

"I remember the day Dad bought you. The real you, that is." She wiped at the dirt and blood and smears on the dolls face, picking bits of grit and dirt from her hair, "I thought you were the prettiest thing I'd ever seen." She felt the warmth of a childish love fill her chest, as the memories came to her, "All those tea parties and picnics we had in the garden, amongst the weeds." She smiled, "It was magical."

She knew that she had taken the wrong approach. She had always healed the toys that came to her, cared for them like soldiers home from war, the way she had never taken care of Pevril. She looked up at the tin soldier as he remounted Clive. Ordering the toys about was never going to work.

*

Crumpet reached out a clawed hand to Sylvia, "Let me through." He said, "*Obbedire.*"

She held herself away from him, while still blocking the doorway. Without being able to touch her, his Charm had no effect.

"You took advantage of me." She said, "You wormed your way into my head, and into my heart, with your black magics. Now look, here we are fighting off the end of the world because of you! ... And because of me."

Crumpet took a step forward, and Sylvia firmly grabbed hold of the door handle, "Come any closer and I'll shut it!"

"If you do that we'll both be trapped." He said, panic rising in his voice.

"Yes." Sylvia nodded, "But I'd rather that than let you back into the world to cause more havoc."

"You don't understand what the Void is, what it would do to a Human mind." Crumpet implored, hands outstretched, his orange eyes wide.

"I don't need to." Sylvia shrugged, "I'm an old lady. I've had a good life. I don't mind spending the last few years of it in some kind of Hell dimension, so long as you do too."

*

"Please forgive me, Pev. I'm sorry," Greta said, as a tear ran down her cheek, "For my part in our little war." She shook her head sadly, "I'm sorry to all of you." This she addressed to the beast at large, or more specifically the toys within it, "I've let you down, letting you be taken over by this Thing. Oh you gorgeous toys, you bringers of wonder. I'll always take you in, and mend your stitching, and plump up your stuffing. I'll fix your limbs, and give you a new lick of paint. I'll make you good as new, so that you can live on to play another day, and to spread the love you're given from one generation to the next. I promise, I'll always be there to take care of you."

She could feel the soles of her feet now merging with her shoes, and the wetness around her, and the flesh of the Everything, "Please." She asked quietly, "Let's not allow this thing to destroy all the joy you bring."

The cavern shook, and the glittering strands of light that hung high above faltered and flickered.

Crumpet looked around desperately, "The conjunction is coming to an end." He said, growing angry, "If we don't go through that door very soon we won't be able to."

The Everything was through the passage, and rearing up to its full height.

"Freedom!" It cawed, and lunged towards the doorway.

Sylvia braced herself, and pulled on the door handle. It swung slowly too, and she turned to face the oncoming beast.

Before it could travel very far, it convulsed, flung sideways by its own twisting shape. It roared as it landed, spit flying into the air from its vibrating lips. Sylvia blinked in astonishment, and spun about to stop the door from closing just in time. Crumpet had also taken the opportunity to make a dash for the door, but Sylvia's bulk stopped him in his tracks. He bounced off of her, and the collision knocked her backwards. She fell through the open door into the swirling darkness.

For a moment she wasn't falling at all. The cavern, the Everything, and Crumpet blinked out, as if someone had turned off the lights. Then she landed in snow, and the sky above her danced with dazzling blue and green light. She squinted, covering her eyes with her hands. She was on Thomas Street, laid on her back in the snow outside the Toy Hospital. Those strange lights were erupting from the roof.

Sitting up, she checked herself over. Still in one piece. Then she looked at the open door in front of her, inside of which was a swirling mass of inky darkness.

"I'm sorry Greta." She said, standing up and making her way to the door. She took hold of it and pushed it shut.

"I am the Everything! Ageless, deathless! From me everything came, and to me everything shall return!" Screamed the convulsing beast.

Crumpet had bashed his head when knocked back from Sylvia, and lay moaning woozily on the ground beside the door. Something was happening to the Everything, something that caused it pain. It seemed to be shrinking, diminishing, deflating.

From somewhere a tinny little voice sang, "All the King's horses and all the King's men, couldn't put Humpty together again!"

Sylvia backed away from the door, her eyes cast up at the lights that continued to pour into the sky above. Her bottom lip quivered, and she began to cry. She had lost her oldest and best friend in all the world. No matter what wrongs she had done in her life, Greta had always done right by her. They had been bosom buddies since their teenage years. But now she was gone, and Sylvia felt suddenly very cold, and very alone, standing in the snow.

As she watched the lights dance into the sky, she wondered why they continued. Shouldn't they have stopped? The door was closed. Why were there still mystical lights erupting from the Toy Hospital roof?

Something shook the Hospital door, and Sylvia's attention snapped to it.

"Oh no." She said, expecting at any moment a giant claw to come bursting through.

It shook, and rattled, and bulged, and erupted open!

"Oh no!" Sylvia couldn't move fast enough, and found herself caught and buried in an avalanche of cheering, happy toys! The tidal wave broke on the shop-fronts opposite, and they flowed, rolling, giggling, gaily in both directions along the street. Sylvia was tossed about, but eventually found her feet, and a handy wall on which to prop herself up. She watched in astonishment as wave after wave of toys broke free of the darkness within the doorway.

"What's happening?" Sylvia wondered, struggling to remain standing as the toys jostled and bundled about her legs.

The wave became a trickle, it seemed the last of the toys were appearing. Then, last of all came a whinnying rocking horse, on the back of which rode Greta Pudding. She clung to the neck of the wooden horse for dear life, with Clive bundled in her lap, and Pevril tangled in her hair.

The rocking horse skidded to a stop, turning sideways-on to Sylvia as it did.

"Greta?" Sylvia was flabbergasted.

Greta blinked, and released her clamped hands from the rocking horse's throat.

"Sylv?" Greta beamed, and threw herself at her friend, hugging her tightly.

Something inside the Toy Hospital went ding and the blackness of the doorway began to flicker, and drain away. The interior slowly came into view as the inky portal swirled and gurgled away into the cupboard.

"What just happened?" Sylvia asked, still clinging tightly to Greta.

Inside the Toy Hospital, the fairy lights flickered into life.

"I think," Greta said, "We might have just saved Christmas."

All about them, the toys of Manchester's toy shops lay in the snow. They were still, and as toys should be.

"Right," Said Sylvia in a back-to-business kind of voice, and releasing her hold of Greta, "What are we going to do about all this mess?"

Someone shouted their names.

Greta and Sylvia turned to see Miss Moss, along with an assortment of other suited individuals wading through the dunes of toys and snow.

The sky began to clear, as the eruption of lights dwindled, dispersed, glittering and rippling into nothing.

"You took your time." Sylvia sniped, rolling her eyes at the Funeral Home employees.

Clive meowed loudly. He wanted kippers.

25th of December.

Sylvia pulled open the brown paper and string to reveal her Christmas present. She made appropriate appreciative noises, flicking through a few pages.

"Thank you, lovey." She said.

"I hate buying pressies." Greta said, "I never know what to get."

"I think it's a lovely gift," Sylvia chuckled, "But maybe we should leave off attempting any occult shenanigans, for a little while at least."

Greta nodded, then turned to Pevril, sat on the arm of the chair beside her, "I've got you a gift as well." She said, "Though I've not had chance to wrap it, what with all the tidying up we had to do yesterday."

He looked at her with his oddly emotive solder-spot eyes.

"Here." Greta said, "Merry Christmas." She presented the tin soldier with a can of WD40 that was bigger than him, "For those squeaky joints of yours."

Pevril leaned against her arm affectionately. It would take some getting used to, having the tin soldier as a friend, rather than enemy. But Sylvia had told her in no uncertain terms that it would be good for her. It would be healing, she had said, to have him around. Greta wasn't sure, but was willing to give it a go, albeit with at least a small show of her usual prickliness, at which Sylvia had simply rolled her eyes.

Clive's Christmas present was some smoked salmon, which he scoffed greedily as soon as it was presented to him. He purred loudly between mouthfuls.

"I've got your gift in my room. Wait there." Sylvia eased herself off of the settee and bashed about noisily in her room for a couple of minutes. She returned dragging a large flat cardboard box, "I hope you like it."

Greta raised a curious eyebrow, as she pulled at the tape that held the box together. The cardboard fell away, and Greta took a gasping breath in.

"The original's paint is all cracked and peeling. So I thought that maybe it was about time for a new one."

Greta admired her present, "It's gorgeous!" She exclaimed.

Sylvia had gifted Greta a brand new sign for the front of the shop. It was a beautiful racing green, with bold gold lettering.

"Toys repaired, resold. Expert care for your beloved toys." Greta read, "Sylv, it's perfect."

"It's double sided," Sylvia grinned sheepishly, "Turn it around."

Greta did so. The reverse was a recreation of the front, with the wording somewhat altered. Greta read it out once more, "Toys possessed? Haunted? Expert care for your bedevilled toys..." She laughed, tutting, "I thought you said we should leave off on occult shenanigans?"

"For a little while. But let's face it, there's no one else who can do what we do."

Greta nodded her agreement.

"Now," Sylvia slapped her hands on her thighs, "I best get the veg started. This dinner won't cook itself, will it?"

*

Miles away from the Toy Hospital, in London, in an unremarkable grey office block, in a drab grey office, Miss Moss sat in a hard plastic chair. Across from her, in a much more comfortable chair, sat a woman so pale she seemed to be made of ice. Her slender fingers grasped the typed report that she was currently scrutinising, and

Crumpet's puzzle box, once more a simple brass cube sat innocuously on the edge of the desk. Standing on a small wooden stand a brass nameplate read Lady G. Shade - Winterfolk Liason.

Miss Moss drummed her nails impatiently on her crossed knees.

"A very interesting report." Said Lady Shade, laying down the sheets of paper and finally looking Miss Moss in the eye, "You continue to demonstrate that you are quite an intrepid and resourceful individual."

"It has been noted more than once." Miss Moss smiled thinly.

"Yet two things stand out to me."

Miss Moss didn't reply, simply waited for the rest of the statement.

"Firstly, your disregard for the chain of command. You took it upon yourself to launch the investigation at the Toy Hospital. Though Gildroy seems to give you leeway to act on your own, I believe that this has encouraged bad habits."

"And secondly?"

"Secondly, your investigation progressed too slowly, leading to the events hazily described by Ms Pudding and Miss Garland."

"The Void seems to have affected their memories. The broad strokes are there, but the details are absent."

Lady Shade gave Miss Moss a sceptical look.

"Ma'am?"

"And thirdly-"

"Oh great, there's more."

"And thirdly, the unforgivable loss of Furious Crumpet to the Abject Void. He has been on our Most Wanted list for decades. Questioning him could have resolved a great many unsolved mysteries, the least of which is how he managed to get a hold of this key." She tapped the brass cube.

"By all accounts it should have been locked away in the vault downstairs." Miss Moss said.

"Quite." Lady Shade scowled.

"Well, consider him sentenced and incarcerated by his own devilish misdemeanours." Miss Moss said, pulling a thread of lint from her skirt.

"Perhaps." The ice-white woman appeared to pause, distracted by a sudden thought, "And there is still the matter of his mysterious employers, that Ms Pudding made mention of."

"I've done a little digging this morning and come up with nothing. I'll get back to it when I'm back in Manchester. I have a few contacts I can squeeze."

"Leave the Crumpet conundrum to me and my team. I have something else in mind for you."

"Disciplinary proceedings, I should imagine."

Smiling, Lady Shade shook her head, "Quite the opposite. Despite your failings you've shown great initiative. I am actually offering you a promotion. You'll still work at the Funeral Home, and perform much the same duties, but I will be your direct superior in all matters of phantasmagorical investigation."

"Mr Silver won't be happy."

"Your first task is to employ your replacement as Gildroy's assistant. I have supplied a list of suitable candidates."

"Yes ma'am."

"And your second task is to bring Ms Pudding and Miss Garland into the fold. As well as that little tin soldier of theirs. They could prove useful assets."

Lady Shade inserted the report into a card file, the front of which was stamped CONFIDENTIAL, Dept. For Ungentlemanly Conduct.

"Now, what do you say?"

"Thank you, aunt Gaudelia."

Lady Shade tutted, "I'm only your aunt when we're not at work. Now run along, it is Christmas after all."

*

Furious Crumpet was finding it harder and harder to hide from the Everything. As the hours and days - how many he couldn't be sure - ticked by and the proximity of the conjunction diminished, the labyrinthine passages of the Abject Void opened out, became wider, untangling themselves from one another. They unspooled into the endless wastes of Elsewhere. Roaring and foaming at what remained of its mouth, the

Everything had hunted him, craving for his atoms to join with its own, and for revenge against someone, anyone, for its defeat!

Crumpet tripped on a loose paving slab and went flying, and didn't land. The walls of the passage around him evaporated into steam, and he tumbled into darkness. All around him he could see the unspooling. The passages, caverns and tunnels unravelling, blooming open like flowers and vanishing. He felt infinitesimally small and insignificant, as the true emptiness of the Void impressed itself upon his consciousness. No living thing should exist in this non-place. And yet, in the distance, tumbling silently towards him, another living thing came; The Everything, and it reached out to grab him.

Also available in this series

Violence & Lavender

When a young runaway is found murdered, it falls to his friends to uncover the truth.

Whispers run rampant, ghostly visitations provide no tangible clues, a Spiritualist does nothing but confuse the situation, and the Police dismiss new evidence and unimportant.

Rowan Forrester is haunted by not just a ghost, but by what could have been, had he ever plucked up the courage to tell the Dear Departed his true feelings.

High society mixes with the queer demimonde of Manchester in the roaring twenties in this vividly textured world populated by vibrant, unforgettable, LGBTQ+ characters.

Pity The Dead

Peter Pretty, orphaned as a baby, finds he has inherited a grand old castle. The corridors twist and turn, someone is scuttling about in secret passages, and a terrible family feud begins to reveal itself.

Then Peter dies.

Forced from their crypt by land development, can Peter's extended family of undead relatives survive in the modern world? And more importantly, can the modern world survive them?

Also available by Rylan John Cavell

Professor Calamity
The Analogue Archive
The PolGnomes and the Vile Grumble
The 'And Other Stories' series

www.rylanjohncavell.com

Printed in Great Britain
by Amazon